POTIONS, POISON, AND PUMPKIN SPICE

Mystic Inn Mysteries

STEPHANIE DAMORE

Chapter 1

____

"Look, but don't look," my best friend and owner of Spellbinding Books said to me.

I glanced over Misty's shoulder out her shop's front window.

"Oh, I thought it was going to be something good." I flicked my gaze away from the new journalist in town. The man's thin lips were pulled down in his ever-present frown. Mr. Haggerty, nicknamed David the Downer by our town's troublesome twins, Sabrina and Beatrice, lifted his clipboard and began furiously scribbling as he critiqued Village Square's decor for his upcoming article on our enchanted town.

Shop owners had decorated the outdoor shopping district with oversized pumpkins, bales of hay, and brightly potted mums. Clemmie had added orange twinkle lights and red and yellow garland made out of leaves to her tea house's display window.

Misty had opted to hire a local muralist to paint a fall scene on her window. Orange and red leaves appeared to fall whimsically into a pile on the ground while a black cat swatted at them in the air.

Next door, Heather had lined the walkway to the diner with solar lanterns. The light inside flickered like a flame after darkness fell.

Mr. Haggerty squatted down and eyed the lanterns like a golfer did when analyzing a putt. He tilted his head.

Misty copied the motion. "Is he seeing if they're in a straight line?" she looked at me incredulously.

"I have no idea what he's doing," I confessed.

Mr. Haggerty stood abruptly and was forced to move off the sidewalk as Chippy Dippy, our resident ice cream man, came strolling down the sidewalk with his ice cream cart.

Dippy used to have a storefront at Village Square until he decided it was too restricting, and he'd rather push an ice cream cart around. When I asked him about it, he said he liked changing his view, and besides, he had just gotten a fitness tracker. He was on a mission to see how many steps he could take in a single day.

Mayor Parrish walked through the door moments later and came to a screeching halt.

"What is this?" she motioned to the front book

display. "True crime? Oh, no, no. This simply won't do. You have to change this. What if Mr. Haggerty sees it? He surely won't approve of such displays of violence."

"I don't think he approves of anything," Misty replied dryly.

Mayor Parrish ignored my best friend's comment. Instead, she rounded on me, "And you."

I took a step back.

"Thelma is in town still, is she not?"

"Er, yes?" I replied more as question versus a statement. I wasn't sure where the mayor was going with her train of thought regarding my aunt, and I wanted to keep my excuses open.

"Then why in the world does the inn look so shabby?"

"Shabby?"

"Two mums? That's all the decorations you have to highlight this town's bicentennial celebration. Two mums! You're not short-staffed, and the town has been doing quite well for itself, I must add. The inn should not be hurting for money. Surely, you have a decorating budget."

Decorating budget? How many businesses had a decorating budget? That's what I wanted to say, but instead, I replied, "Oh, I was going for understated elegance."

"Nothing about this weekend can be understated. Must I remind you that Silverlake is up for the prestigious Best Fall Getaway Award from *Witch Reader's Magazine*? We will not lose to the snooty town of Fallspell again. Do you hear me?"

Misty and I looked at one another before quickly agreeing with the mayor.

"Now see to it the inn looks freshened up and get rid of this display. How about you showcase something more cheerful? Or better yet, highlight the town's rich history." Mayor Parrish left with a flourish after that, not bothering to say goodbye.

"I think she's officially lost her mind," Misty replied.

"I think she's just stressed."

"I get that she wants to win, but I don't think it's going to happen. Did you hear what happened at the tavern last night?"

"No. Haven't you learned by now that I never know what's happening? I rely on you and Clemmie to fill me in."

"Forget I asked. All you need to know is Mr. Haggerty got a little tipsy on fire whiskey, and next thing you know, the journalist was running his mouth about how pathetic our town is."

"Are you sure? He doesn't even look like the drinking type." I eyed Mr. Haggerty through the window and watched him adjust the buttons on his cuff links.

"He said our town was driving him to drink." Misty raised her eyebrows.

"Why would he say such a thing?"

"I guess he's not too happy with his editor for sending him here. He was supposed to go to the Wine Country." Misty mimicked Mr. Haggerty's snooty attitude as she said the last part. "The man better hope it doesn't rain because with his nose so far up in the air, he's sure to drown."

I laughed because it was true. Mr. Haggerty was staying at the inn, and I'd lost count of how many times he'd called down to the front desk. Last time, he requested spring water ice cubes and warm bath towels. Apparently, the ice machine and standard bathroom towels weren't adequate.

"And then Amber was there," Misty rolled her eyes, referring to my high school arch-enemy and local deputy. "She wanted to arrest him on the spot for being disrespectful."

"Of course she did."

"And you know you can't do that. Freedom of speech and all that, but it took Craig Daniels seeing Mr. Haggerty home to get Amber to back off."

I shook my head. Mr. Haggerty was lucky the tavern owner was there to call Amber off. Amber and her daddy, the sheriff, were always the type to arrest first and ask questions later.

"Do you think Amber will ever learn?" I asked.

"Probably not. But we can keep hoping." Misty eyed her true crime display once more. "Guess I better get to rearranging these books."

"Want some help?"

"No, that's okay. I'm only going to switch tables. After this weekend, these books are back to center stage."

"Nice. I guess I better get going, then. I'm going to walk over to Roger's and see what other fall flowers he has in stock." Roger was married to my good friend, Diane. He always had beautiful arrangements. We had already pulled the geraniums out of the window boxes, and I guess if I thought about it, it did make the front of the inn look rather dull. At the time, I had felt the surrounding fall foliage made up for the inn's bare exterior, but maybe Mayor Parrish was right. There was no harm in stopping by the flower shop and seeing what Roger could do.

Chapter 2

I said goodbye to Misty and headed out the bookshop's back door, picking up the flagstone path that connected the shops of Village Square. As I walked, I couldn't help but pick up on the town's cozy atmosphere. All around me, locals greeted one another and offered the same warm smiles to visitors as they opened their shop doors or passed one another on the sidewalk. Bright-colored orange and red leaves floated down from the trees as a soft breeze rippled through the air. And when the direction was just right, you could smell the wood smoke filter across the lake from the campground. Fall could be hit or miss down south, but this year's proved to be unseasonably cooler. It was a welcome respite from the sweltering summer heat. I tucked my long cable-knit blue sweater across my body and folded my arms across my chest to keep it closed.

"Morning, where you off to?" My aunt's best friend, Clemmie, hollered from her tea shop. She was out front sweeping the leaves off of her porch.

"Headed to see Roger about some flowers," I hollered back.

"Woo-ee! Does this mean you're getting married?"

I smiled and shook my head. It was no secret that Vance and I were engaged, but we hadn't set a date for the wedding. "No, not yet. I need some new plants or flowers for the front of the inn." I motioned with my head toward the general direction of Mystic Inn.

Clemmie waved my comment away with one hand while the other hand held onto the broomstick. "Tell Mayor Parrish you don't have time for her nonsense." Clemmie knew exactly where the suggestion had come from.

"Maybe next time," I added over my shoulder as I picked up my pace. The town had several events planned for the bicentennial celebration. Tonight was a parade. It ended at the high school where there'd be a bonfire and an outdoor carnival. Tomorrow night was the formal gala where Silverlake was going to unveil our famous sapphire that gave our town its magical protection. Finally, the town would come together on Sunday for a chili cook-off and picnic. Mayor Parrish had wanted something fancier, but her constituents won out in the end, and she was forced to concede. Vance was adamant he would win, as were Clemmie, Mr. McCormick, and my friend Luke, the candy maker. In fact, everyone I knew who was entering thought they had the best chili recipe. I was happy I wasn't judging the contest. I'd much rather be a taste tester.

I walked through the flower shop's front door and was immediately greeted by the overpowering sweet scent of fresh-cut flowers mixed with something spicier. Identifying the exact scent was quickly forgotten when I took in the dozens of centerpieces filling every available counter space in Roger's small shop. The centerpieces weren't large. You could easily carry them with two hands. But they were striking. In the center was a rich black orchid with bold red centers. Pops of orange, red, and yellow from additional flowers played off one another, creating a magical fall centerpiece all housed in a shallow glass base. I mindlessly walked over to the centerpieces and took a closer look, completely entranced with their beauty.

"Roger, these are gorgeous," I said over my shoulder as he came out from the back with more of the orchids. "The mayor must love them."

"You would think so, but she asked that I make them taller." Roger sighed as if that was the last thing he wanted to do.

"Taller? I wouldn't change a thing. I hate when people make centerpieces so tall that it's impossible to talk across the table. These are the perfect height, and they look amazing. You are so talented."

"Thank you, Angelica. After today, it's nice to hear someone say so."

"Don't feel too bad. Mayor Parrish critiqued the inn as well. That's why I'm here. Do you have any idea of what I could put in the front plant boxes to give the inn a bit of a fall face-lift? And I'm thinking it better not be mums, or who knows what Mayor Parrish might do."

"She didn't threaten you with an engorgement charm, did she?" Roger asked.

"She threatened you?"

"Not me, but the centerpieces. I'm thinking about waiting until later tomorrow to deliver them when she's too busy fussing about something else to give me too much grief."

"That's not a bad plan." I'd probably wait until the last minute to deliver them too.

"Now, about your flower boxes. I have some smaller arrangements in the refrigerator I put together for the hospital. I designed them to grow in the basket, but what I think you should do, is go pay a visit to Mike McCormick."

I knew Mr. McCormick very well. He was one of Silverlake's most active town council members, and his daughter Molly and I had gone to school together. He was a great guy, and he also happened to own the town's greenhouse. "I stopped by his place the other day, and he has some great coneflower plants. Beautiful colors with pink, yellow, and orange. It would liven up the inn better than anything I have."

"That's a great idea. Maybe I'll take a quick drive out there and see what I can find."

"Good luck. If you need anything else, I'll be here working." Roger took in all the centerpieces he had completed. His weariness seemed to indicate he couldn't wait for tomorrow's gala to be over.

I turned around to leave when the shop's door opened, and in walked Cassidy Piper. She had recently opened a homeopathic store in town after our beloved healer, Constantine, had decided to retire to the mountains of North Carolina with her sister.

"Hello Angelica, how are you doing?" Cassidy asked.

"Good, and you?"

"Can't complain. Well, I suppose I could with how slow business has been, but I'm hopeful things will pick up once word of my remedies gets around."

"And I'm sure it will. That tonic of yours straightened my arthritis out right away." Roger flexed his fingers to show how easily he could open and close his palm.

"I'm so happy to hear that." Cassidy turned to Roger with a smile on her face.

"Now, what can I do for you?" Roger asked.

"I was getting ready to put in a flower order from my distributor and thought I'd check in with you and see if maybe you wanted to split shipping together?"

"That's not a bad idea," Roger replied.

I waved goodbye to the duo and let them continue their business while seeing myself out the door.

Chapter 3

I ended up gabbing with Mr. McCormick longer than I thought I would, but when I arrived back at the inn an hour and a half later, the back seat of Aunt Thelma's Buick was chock full of fall plants. Not only would Mayor Parrish be pleased with the inn's refreshed look, but I was sure our guests would be as well. The inn would look nice all the way until it was time to decorate for Christmas.

"Welcome to Silverlake. You're going to love it here," Aunt Thelma said to a woman and young girl who appeared to be checking in. Both women had shoulder-length, strawberry-blonde hair, and I'd bet my wand that they were related.

"We hope so, don't we?" The woman brushed the girl's hair off her shoulder and looked lovingly down at her.

"Oh, here's my niece now. Angelica, meet Silverlake's newest residents. Jane and her daughter, Amelia."

"Nice to meet you." I waved as I moved to join my aunt behind the front counter.

"I was telling them that once you live in Silverlake, you'll always consider it home. Isn't that right?"

"Very true," I agreed.

Jane was a mortal, meaning she had no magical spark. You could tell by the way her body faintly glowed. I hadn't meant to stare, but we didn't get many mortals here. Nonmagical folks usually didn't know about Silverlake. The duo's presence was a mystery in itself.

"I know, I'm glowing." The woman held up her palms in front of her and examined them. "I can't see it, but I remember coming here as a child. The gift skips a generation, you see." Jane swallowed uncomfortably. "It's just, my mother thought Silverlake might be more accepting." The woman gave a sad smile. There was more to the story, but now wasn't the time to pry. It seemed to be a delicate matter involving her daughter.

"Your mother was right. Everyone's welcome in Silverlake," Aunt Thelma chimed in, breaking the somber atmosphere.

"That they are," I replied with a smile.

"We heard there's a fancy party tomorrow night. Are we invited?" Amelia asked.

"Amelia!" Jane admonished her daughter.

"Of course, you're invited. The whole town is!" Aunt Thelma exclaimed.

"Ooooooh, can we go, mom?" Amelia looked hopefully up at her mom.

"I don't know. We'll see."

"That means no," Amelia said to the ground.

Jane sighed. "Where's the party at?"

Amelia's face perked up.

"It's at city hall on the other side of the lake, right in the center of the business district. I can give you directions. It's pretty easy to find," I said. Especially if Mayor Parrish rolled out the red carpet like she planned to.

"And you'll be able to see the Silverlake Sapphire. That's the enchanted gemstone that gives our town its magical power," Aunt Thelma added excitedly. After much deliberation, the town council had decided to put the sapphire on display. I still wasn't sure it was a good idea. On one hand, putting it out in the open took some of the mystery away. Maybe if people could see it, they wouldn't try to hunt it down anymore. On the other hand, it was very valuable, both in monetary value and for our town. The sapphire was what kept Silverlake safe from the outside world. Unfortunately, its value is what made it a target for thefts. There really was no right answer.

Amelia's face instantly shifted from excitement

to worry. Her eyes zoned out, and she appeared lost in space.

"What's wrong?" Jane looked down at her daughter. "Amelia?"

It took a moment for the young girl to snap out of it. "I don't think displaying the sapphire is such a good idea. I think someone might try to steal it." Amelia looked up at her mother. Jane wore an equally worried expression, but I had a feeling it was more because of Amelia's prediction rather than worry about the sapphire.

"Can you see the future?" I asked.

"Mm-hmm. I'm really good at it. Aren't I, mom?"

"Eh..." Jane rubbed her temples as if she was getting a headache. Raising a daughter was hard enough. Raising one coming into her psychic powers only made things harder.

"Are you sure you're not picking up on past events? Someone did try to steal it this past summer," Aunt Thelma confessed.

"Maybe," the young girl shrugged. "But the wedding I'm picking up on is definitely in the future." The girl's brow furrowed.

"What wedding?" I asked.

"Your wedding," the girl said as if that was obvious. Her expression darkened once more. Her mother squeezed her shoulder and shook her head as if telling her daughter not to say anything else.

Amelia cleared her throat. "It's nothing. Is our room ready? I want to charge my phone before tonight."

Aunt Thelma handed over her room key and gave the duo instructions to their guest room while I stood there wondering what the young psychic had seen.

"I wouldn't worry about it," Aunt Thelma said after Jane and Amelia were out of earshot.

"What? Oh, I'm not." I shook my head and looked back toward the parking lot. I still had to tackle the decorations.

"Is everything okay, dear? I was getting a bit worried about you." Aunt Thelma looked down at her wrist as if she was wearing a watch. "Fiddle-sticks. That's right; I lost my watch. Anyway, I thought you'd be back hours ago."

"Sorry, I first went and visited Roger to talk about flowers—"

"Finally! You and Vance set a date!" Aunt Thelma cut me off with her excitement.

"No. You're just as bad as Clemmie. I went and visited Roger after Mayor Parrish thought we could use a little bit more fall decor, and he sent me to Mr. McCormick, who hooked us up. I have enough plants in the back of the car to last until Christmas."

"But have you and Vance thought about setting a date?" Aunt Thelma walked toward the little kitchenette and returned carrying a tray of muffins.

"Are those muffins cranberry? Don't let Mayor

Parrish see. She might fine you for lack of pumpkin spice."

"Pish posh. The only place I like pumpkin spice is in my pie. And don't change the subject. Are you guys any closer to picking a date?"

"We've tried, but honestly, every time one of us suggests one, the other has a reason it won't work, and neither of us has time to plan a wedding." I didn't want to make Aunt Thelma feel bad, but with her spending half the year with her boyfriend, Frederick, in Mount Holly, and with Silverlake becoming more touristy, I didn't have time to plan a wedding and run the inn full-time. As far as I knew, there wasn't a spell to clone a witch, but I wished there was. "I don't know; maybe we'll just elope." Not that either one of us wanted to, but we also didn't want to wait another year to get married. Vance and I were ready to tie the knot. We just hadn't had a ton of time to plan. I'd started a binder of ideas, and we knew we wanted to get married in Silverlake surrounded by all our friends, but that was it.

"You know, I could plan your wedding," Aunt Thelma offered.

I blinked my response.

"What, you don't think I could do it? I can picture it now: a lovely church wedding, beautiful flowers, soft candlelight. We'd follow it up with an intimate dinner with plenty of delicious food, laughter, and of course, cake. Cheesecake, if I'm not mistaken. It's always been both your favorite.

I stood with my mouth open because that did sound perfect. "How did you know?"

"Because I know my niece. So, what do you say? Am I your official wedding planner?"

It took me a minute to find my voice. "Sure. I guess so. Let me just double-check with Vance." "

"Check in with me about what?" I hadn't even noticed Vance walk into the lobby.

"Leave everything to me," Aunt Thelma patted Vance on the shoulder as she strolled past him into the office.

"What's going on? It's never a good thing when your aunt's eyes twinkle like that."

"She wants to plan the wedding."

"Our wedding?" Vance motioned between the two of us.

"Mm-hmm."

"What do you think about that?" he asked.

"I think it might be a good idea. We clearly don't have the time. What do you think?"

"I'm good with it if you are. I just want to make sure you get exactly what you want."

"You mean what we want."

"No, I definitely mean you. I'd marry you right here and now if I could."

"As much as I love hearing that, I do want a nice

wedding." I thought for a moment. "And I think Aunt Thelma can make it happen."

"Then it sounds like we've hired a wedding planner."

I exhaled a breath, feeling the weight lift off my chest. I hadn't realized how stressed I'd been trying to figure everything out. "I'll let Aunt Thelma know. But first, can you help me with some plants? Then we can catch up with her and head to the parade."

"Sure, I can do that."

It was easier said than done.

Vance stopped and stared when he took in the back seat of the car. It was like a forest witch had taken over the inside and cast an autumn foliage spell. "I'm surprised you were able to see out the back window while driving."

I grimaced. "I wasn't. But it wasn't like I had to drive very far. Come on, help me out."

Vance and I lugged every potted plant, ornamental planter, and wreath out of the car. Mr. McCormick had put trash bags down on the back seat to protect the fabric, but it hadn't been foolproof. Some dirt managed to spill out and streak across the seats, staining the gray upholstery. Vance went to withdraw his wand.

"Wait, I got it. I've been practicing. You're about to be impressed." I withdrew my wand from my back pocket and cleared my throat. There was a time, not too long ago, when I was hesitant to use magic. I thought there was nothing practical about it. So much has changed since then. I'm now proud to be a witch with a few tricks up her sleeve.

I confidently pointed my wand at the back seat and commanded, "Rochí."

Water gushed out of the tip of my wand like a fire hose on full blast. My hand shot up from the force, spraying the ceiling before I whipped around and soaked Vance instead. His hands reached out to try to stop the onslaught. Instead of dropping the wand or shouting a counter curse, all I could do was stare in shock.

"Tixie!" Vance hollered on my behalf. Seeing it wasn't his spell, it didn't stop the water. But what it did do was bring me to my senses, and I repeated the counter curse after him. The water ceased immediately—the last remnants disappearing into the air.

My mouth was wide open as I looked at Vance in shock. " I'm so sorry." I couldn't keep the laughter out of my voice.

"Are you laughing? You're laughing at me right now, aren't you?" Vance wasn't upset. He was just giving me a hard time.

"Here, let me fix it." I raised my wand and shouted out the spell for wind. Aunt Thelma had taught it to me recently. It made drying your hair a breeze. Except now, a gust of wind shot out of my wand so forcefully, Vance tumbled backward, tripping onto the sidewalk.

This time I was much quicker to lower my wand and extinguish the spell. All humor was gone. I rushed forward to give Vance a hand up. "I'm so sorry. I have no idea what's going on." It used to be that I didn't remember enough spells to be an effective witch, and my powers were bound, but now it was as if my powers had grown too strong. I still couldn't control them. Either way, I was a walking disaster.

"Remind me not to make you mad," Vance brushed off the back of his pant. His shirt was still soaked.

I winced. "I really am sorry."

"I know you are. You were only trying to help."

"But I should keep my wand pointed at myself for now?"

"I didn't say that."

"No, but you should." I bit my bottom lip in frustration. I knew Vance wasn't mad at me, but I still felt awful about releasing the elements on him. At least I hadn't set him on fire. Maybe I should quit doing magic altogether. It might be the best way to keep people safe. That thought left me feeling depressed. Despite the vibrant colors, my mood was starting to get gray.

"Hey, don't do that. Don't beat yourself up.

Look at me." I flicked my eyes at Vance. "You're a good witch. We'll figure this out."

"It's fine, don't worry about it." I didn't need to make Vance feel sorry for me, and I didn't want to make this a big deal and ruin our night. I cleared my throat. "Do you want to go home and change while I arrange the plants?"

"How about I run inside and conjure some clothes from my apartment? It'll be quicker, and they're probably closing off the road soon."

"You're right. That's a better idea."

Fifteen minutes later, the front of the inn looked lovely, even if I wasn't feeling so festive.

"What has you so down, dear?" Aunt Thelma said when I entered the lobby.

"Did you see what I did to Vance? He's lucky I didn't hurt him."

"Oh, don't worry about it. He seemed to take it in good stride."

"This time. I don't know what's going on. Maybe I'm not a very good witch."

"Hush now. No descendent of mine is going to talk that way. What you need is a bit of polishing up, and I have just the idea." I looked warily at my aunt, waiting for her to continue. "Magic school, my dear."

"Magic school?" Silverlake taught magic as part of the school curriculum, but there was no way I was going back to high school. I graduated years ago. "Mount Holly has a wonderful school that focuses just on the magical arts. The headmistress is about your age."

"Aunt Thelma, I can't run off to Mount Holly and learn magic."

"Well, now let me finish. I'm thinking that maybe Vanessa could send the course materials to you. Like an independent study. You guys could even meet online. What's that called again?"

"Video conferencing?"

"Yes, that's it. Do you know you can see people anywhere around the world if they have an Internet connection? And I thought I was powerful."

"I'll think about it."

"I can reach out to Vanessa, too. Or if you'd like," Aunt Thelma continued, her eyes brightening, "I could be your tutor. It wasn't right of me to run off to Mount Holly so quickly after you came back. I should've stayed and been here for you."

I was quick to put that line of thought to an end. Aunt Thelma did not need to delay her happiness to care for me. I was a grown woman. Which reminded me just how much I needed to stop feeling sorry for myself and get hold of my magic. I had talked about wanting to take a refresher course before, and how many books had I checked out from the library and bought from Misty on the subject? Maybe it was time that I had a tutor.

"How about I reach out to Vanessa? Do you have her contact info?"

Aunt Thelma clapped her hands together. "Wonderful. A couple of courses of Vanessa's, and you will be brimming with confidence."

Vance came down a few moments later wearing dark jeans and a light blue button-down. A black windbreaker was draped over his arm as he held his other hand toward me to take.

"Are you sure you're okay?" I said as my fingers slipped through his.

"Promise." Vance brought my hand to his lips and gave it a quick kiss before lowering our hands once more. "It was an accident. They happen to the best of us. Are you ready to head out?" Vance changed the subject, and I let him.

"Yes, let me go get my coat."

"Did you hear about all the food trucks that will be there? I didn't know we had so many in Silverlake now," Aunt Thelma chimed in.

"I know, from the sounds of it, the high school parking lot will be full of them. I can't wait." It used to be that we had one or two food trucks that would hang out around the business district at lunchtime. That soon grew to a few more and a few more. Last I heard, the town council was talking about allowing the food trucks to set up in the church parking lot on weekdays, giving them a centralized location. No more having to track the trucks on a map and hope they hadn't moved before you got there.

"You guys head out. I'll meet you at the high school afterward," Aunt Thelma said.

"Are you sure you don't want to ride with us? There's plenty of room." The road around the back side of the lake stayed open the entire parade.

"No need. I'm picking up Clemmie, and together we're going to make sure tonight's bonfire burns bigger and brighter than ever before. That is, as long as I can find my wand." Aunt Thelma patted her pockets and looked in front and behind her.

I shook my head. My dear aunt was always losing things. "Do you want some help looking for it?"

Aunt Thelma held her finger up in a eureka moment and dashed into the little kitchenette off the lobby and came back with a bowl full of pretzels. Her wand was sticking out of it. She plucked it out of the bowl and held it up triumphantly. "My hands were full, and I meant to carry them out together. Disaster averted. Now I'll see you guys in a little bit."

Chapter 4

Vance and I found a spot on the sidewalk that wasn't too crowded to stand and wave as members of Silverlake paraded by. The marching band played a rendition of Michael Jackson's Thriller, with the school spirit squad dressed up as zombies, performing the iconic dance moves in sync with the music. Our town's littlest witches performed a separate routine as they marched past, cheering with their orange and green metallic pom-poms. The Simmering Sisters even participated. The ladies in the cooking club had donned pointed witch's hats and purple aprons as they passed out packaged sugar cookies and brownies. A few other members walked down the middle of the road with a large bowl tucked under one arm and a whisk in the other. A steady stream of purple smoke floated out of their bowls, smelling impressively like chocolate chip cookies. Whatever that spell was, it would be torture if you were on a diet. I eyed the brownie Vance had, suddenly wanting to trade.

"Switch you," I held the sugar cookie out.

"How about we split fifty-fifty?" Vance countered.

"That's an even better plan." Vance and I opened our goodies, and I broke the cookie in half and passed him over a chunk.

"You know what would go good with this," I said after swallowing a bite of buttery frosted goodness.

Vance looked at me, and at the same time, we said, "Coffee."

"Doesn't Diane have a booth over at the high school?" Vance reminded me.

"You're right. Mayor Parrish insisted she sell pumpkin spice lattes, but knowing Diane, I'm sure she's offering up more than that." We could see the food trucks from where we were watching the parade, but what we couldn't see was all the other vendors set up around the perimeter. Diane was selling baked goods and hot drinks. The high school's PTO was selling licensed apparel. It looked mostly like sweatshirts and blankets in the school colors and embroidered with the mascot. A smart move seeing the air was getting colder, and wrapping up with a blanket while standing around the town's bonfire sounded like a cozy idea. I also spotted my friend Luke, the owner of the Candy

Cauldron, along with his nieces, Sabrina and Beat-rice. The witches were offering up free samples of chocolates. I shied away from the troublesome twosome. No offense to Luke, but it would take a lot for me to trust anything the girls were passing out. I didn't want to turn orange, grow a tail, or anything else they came up with. But plenty of other folks seemed eager to try their latest creation. From what I could see, they looked like truffles with a glossy bright green exterior. I could only guess the flavor. Sour apple, maybe? Beatrice retrieved a second tray. This batch had a colorful purple coating.

"I'm almost tempted," I said to Luke as we passed by. I pointed down at Beatrice's tray.

Luke chuckled. "I don't blame you for being worried, but they're really good. I've already had three, and I promise you I haven't had smoke come out of my ears or anything."

"What flavors are they?" Vance asked the girls.

Sabrina took the lead. "The green ones have a key lime and coconut center covered in a graham cracker shell and then coated in white chocolate." She sounded like a professional chocolatier.

"And the purple ones are salted caramel cashew with layers of milk and white chocolate," Beatrice added. The young witches beamed with pride.

"We had pumpkin spice ones too, but Mayor Parrish bought all of them," Sabrina added.

"Wow, I'm impressed. Those do sound good," I replied.

"Do you want to try one?" the girls asked in unison. I couldn't very well say no now, could I? "We promise we didn't curse them or anything," Beatrice added.

"Promise. We only used fair trade, non-GMO ingredients."

"Only the best."

"We're making a name for ourselves. Uncle Luke here isn't going to live forever," Sabrina looked solemnly at Luke.

"Then somebody's gonna have to run his business." Beatrice nodded.

"Nothing like children to remind you of your mortality," Luke spoke above them. "The girls have been apprenticing with me since summer. I find that if I give them something constructive to do, there's less destruction. So far, they've been quick learners."

"Uncle Luke says we're naturals."

"How about I try one of the key lime coconut ones?" I suggested.

"And I'll try the salted caramel," Vance said.

I hoped I wasn't making a mistake as my teeth cracked the soft outer shell and sunk into the smooth middle. "Oh my goodness, this is good." I put my hand over my mouth while I spoke. "Girls, this is impressive. I think your uncle's right."

"I'd say so. You have a future in the chocolatier business." Vance added.

The girls beamed with pride. "Great! We're selling them in four or six packs if you'd like. You can see Ben at the stand, and he'll ring you up."

My eyebrows shot up. "They're good in sales, too."

Luke shook his head. "Don't feel obligated."

"No, no, it's fine. The chocolates are good. Happy to support you guys," I said to the girls. We said goodbye to them, purchased six truffles, and headed farther down the line.

"That was surprising," Vance remarked.

"I know. Hopefully, their mischievous days are behind them." Their mom worked full-time as a nurse at the community hospital on the other side of the lake, and she only had her brother to help with the girls. Luke was always more than willing to help, telling me that they were all the family he had. They always stuck together.

"Who's this?" Vance asked, motioning to the next booth before us. It was hard to make out the words at first with all the glitter and stickers on the posterboard sign, but as we got closer, I could see it read, "Fortunes $5".

A line had formed behind the booth where Amelia confidently told Misty her fortune while her mother fidgeted nervously beside her.

"That's Amelia and her mother, Jane. They just

moved to Silverlake and are staying at the inn until they can get settled."

"And she's a psychic?"

I wanted to say that I hoped not, given the look she shared with her mother when she brought up our wedding, but who knows what she was going to say. By the length of the line quickly growing behind her booth, I assumed the young girl had to be somewhat gifted.

Misty joined us with a scowl on her face.

"What's wrong?" I asked.

"I wasted five bucks. That's what's wrong."

"What did she say?"

"That I'll have my heart broken, which is just dumb. Everything is going great with Daniel. He's supposed to return from Prague in two weeks, and we're planning to spend some downtime together."

"Maybe she didn't mean Daniel?" I offered, hopefully.

"Who else would break my heart?"

"She might just be making it up," Vance suggested.

"I don't know. That's the part that bothers me. You could feel the magic coming off of her. That little girl knows her stuff," Misty scowled. "It's just my luck. I fall for a guy, and then he dumps me. Why do I even bother?"

"He's not going to dump you!" I wanted to shake my best friend silly.

"Whatever. See if I care. I don't need Daniel to make me happy."

Vance opened his mouth to say something. I subtly shook my head.

"Now that I'm officially depressed, I'm going to see how many cupcakes Diane has. I'll see you guys later."

"Wow. Overreact much?" Vance said to Misty's retreating form.

"Just a bit. She'll calm down. I'm sure of it." Especially after she caught up with Daniel.

"It looks like your aunt and Clemmie really got the fire going." Vance motioned to the grassy area between the parking lot and the football field, where a bright blue and orange fire blazed. In the off-season, the area was the soccer field, but tonight it housed the community bonfire. Mr. McCormick told me all about how the town council had laid the fire pit, brick by brick, and tomorrow they would work on disassembling it once the bricks had cooled. Townsmen had already gathered around the fire to cast their spells. The way it worked was you were supposed to write something you regretted on a piece of paper, something you wanted to let go of. Then you crumbled up the piece of paper and threw it in the fire, making a wish on the smoke as it rose into the air.

Did I have any current regrets? That's what I was trying to think about. Sure, I regretted leaving

Silverlake and giving up magic, but I was already making peace with that. Then there was Vance and my relationship. Talk about regret. Neither one of us had been very mature all those years ago.

The better question would be, what do I want to let go of? The answer suddenly came to me. I wanted to let go of being afraid of failure, of never mastering my magic, and continuously making a fool of myself. I needed to let go of feeling inadequate and like I'd never live up to my Nightingale heritage. My dream was that I would step into all my powers and continue to open myself up to the possibilities. I wanted to love freely and wholly. I wanted to build a family with Vance. To get married and settle down in Silverlake for years to come. I wanted to stitch together a beautiful life, one day at a time.

"Hello? Earth to Angie?" Vance had been talking, and I wasn't paying any attention. "I guess you have a lot of regrets?" Vance suddenly looked unsure of everything.

"Not regrets. But there are things I want to let go of and dreams I want to reach for. Good things," I quickly clarified. "Dreams for us, our future, and what that looks like." I took a deep breath and let the cool evening air fill my lungs. "I'm so happy that I came home, and yet I still feel like I'm punishing myself for the past. I want to let go of all that and live in the now. That's all."

"I want that for you too. For us. C'mon, let's head to the fire."

Vance and I hadn't made it very far when Mr. Haggerty caught our eye. He seemed to be arguing with Mayor Parrish.

"That doesn't look good." I hadn't even noticed the journalist had shown up to the high school, but there he was, standing next to the Terry Dawes stand. The rough and tough shifter recently started selling jerky. I heard Terry used to make it out of his home and pass it out to coworkers on the road crew, but he'd since started selling it at local shops. I hadn't paid much attention when we'd passed by the stand the first time, but tonight Terry was also selling raw meat on the stick that you could roast in the fire. It was a twist on roasting hotdogs over a fire. By the looks of the number of people snacking on meat sticks, the idea wasn't only a hit with shifters. Everyone seemed to love the idea except for Mr. Haggerty.

"I've never seen something so barbaric!" Mr. Haggerty snapped.

"That seems a bit harsh." Mayor Parrish tilted her head from side to side as she tried to weigh her words. "Look around. Everyone's enjoying it. We have shifters, which is —"

"Talk about disgusting things," Mr. Haggerty said, not bothering to hide his contempt.

"Now, what is that supposed to mean?"

"What's next, vampires?"

"We do have a vampire pop in from time to time," Mayor Parrish started to say until she realized that was exactly the wrong reply.

"*Witch Reader's Magazine* is for witches. We don't cater to shifters, vampires, or any other half-blood, supernatural creature you have roaming around here."

"Pardon me?"

"I've seen enough. Silverlake is not the right fit for this award."

"Now, wait a moment. Please. Wait until the gala tomorrow night before making up your mind. I promise you will be impressed."

"You couldn't pay me enough to stay. Good evening and goodbye." Mr. Haggarty stomped off, leaving Mayor Parrish distraught.

"How could he say such awful things about Silverlake? And everyone that lives here? I'm just speechless."

"I say good riddance. I know how hard you worked to please Mr. Haggerty, but do we want an award if it comes from the likes of him?" I asked.

"Well, I thought it would be a nice addition to the town's website." Mayor Parrish swallowed nervously. "Oh, what am I going to tell everyone?"

"I wouldn't say anything," Vance added.

"Vance is right. This weekend wasn't about

trying to win an award. It's about honoring Silver-lake. We should be focusing on that."

"Oh, I suppose you're right. It just puts a damper on things. I am downright depressed."

That seemed to be a common theme tonight, I thought to myself, recalling Misty. "I heard Diane has pumpkin spice lattes," I offered, thinking that might cheer the mayor up.

"If I drink one more pumpkin spice latte or eat one more pumpkin spice truffle, it'll be too soon. Hopefully, Diane has some strong black coffee. I need it."

"I'm sure she does." I hoped she did, anyhow.

"I'll catch up with the two of you later." Mayor Parrish didn't move. Instead, she shook her head and suddenly looked as if she might cry.

"What, what is it?" I rubbed the mayor's shoulder.

"I was thinking how truly awful that Mr. Haggerty is. I, for one, hope he never returns. Rotten, rotten, man." Mayor Parrish thrust her finger in the air as if she was making a declaration and then turned and marched off.

Chapter 5

Thankfully, the rest of the evening passed by uneventfully. The evening was rather enjoyable without Mr. Haggerty present and Amelia no longer telling fortunes. The marching band booster club passed out s'mores-making kits, and the French club gave out complimentary hot chocolate. I did buy one of the blankets at the PTO booth and snuggled with Vance around the fire while hanging out with Diane and Roger, Clemmie, Luke, and Aunt Thelma. I wasn't sure where Misty had run off to, but hopefully, it was to catch up with Daniel.

Mayor Parrish also disappeared early, and I couldn't blame her. She had put in a lot of work trying to make Silverlake everything Mr. Haggerty wanted it to be. I knew she had been disappointed, but in my opinion, Mr. Haggerty turned out to be the type of man who didn't deserve to be impressed.

As I replayed some of his comments, I couldn't believe half of the things he said, especially the digs about shifters and vampires. His prejudice and poor attitude made me consider reaching out to the magazine's managing editor. Nothing good might come out of it, especially if the editor was anything like Mr. Haggerty. Still, if I was running a magazine, I would want to know if my reporters were disrespecting people and making the publication look bad.

The next morning, I was online looking up the editor's contact information when Eleanor, Percy the Poltergeist's wife and head housekeeper, approached me. The inn had never been cleaner since she took over.

"Canceling your subscription?" Eleanor said once she realized what website I was on.

"Something like that. What can I do for you?"

"It's about Mr. Haggerty."

"Don't tell me he trashed his room." He didn't seem like the type, but I had come to expect the unexpected in this business. People didn't respect hotel rooms.

"I'm not sure. The thing is, he hasn't checked out yet."

I looked up at the clock. It was going on noon. Checkout time was eleven o'clock.

"I was trying to be respectful of his privacy and keep out of the room, but I'd appreciate it if he could leave sooner rather than later. We have a full house tonight."

"You're right. We do." Confronting Mr. Haggerty was the last thing I wanted to do, but Eleanor had a point. We did have a full house tonight, which meant she had plenty of work to do. "I'll go see what's keeping him."

Eleanor followed me down the hall to the last room on the right. It was a ground-floor suite that overlooked the lake. Mayor Parrish had insisted I reserve the best room for Mr. Haggerty. No amenity was to be spared. In hindsight, I don't think it would've mattered what room I had reserved for the gentleman. Nothing would have pleased him.

"Mr. Haggerty?" I knocked on the door and waited a few moments before knocking again. "Mr. Haggerty, it's Angelica Nightingale. Do you need any help checking out?" I looked at Eleanor. She raised her translucent blue shoulders as if to say she had no clue what was keeping him.

"I'll just take a quick peek," Eleanor whispered as she proceeded to stick her head through the wood door. I guess there were some benefits to being a ghost. Eleanor must not have been able to see Mr. Haggerty because a moment later, her entire body slipped through the door. I waited impatiently for her to return, trying to hear what was happening. I thought I heard Eleanor say something, but I couldn't be sure what she said.

My ear was pressed up to the door when the ghost came flying back through in a hurry. The coldness of Eleanor's body slammed into mine, and it felt as if she'd drenched me with a bucket of ice water. The coldness sucked my breath away, and I stumbled backward with an intense brain freeze. I squinted my eyes shut, hating the feeling, and exhaled, hoping the warmth of my breath would take a bit of the chill away.

"I'm so sorry. I didn't mean to run into you, but you need to get in here right away. Something is wrong with Mr. Haggerty!"

"Hang on, let me grab a key." I wasted no time getting a key for Mr. Haggarty's room, and I quickly followed Eleanor inside.

"Mr. Haggerty?" The man was lying face down on the carpet. He had a cup of coffee in his hand with a lid on it. The beverage had spilled out, soaking into the carpet.

"Mr. Haggerty?" I jostled his shoulder, but he didn't even flinch. My fingers quickly searched for a pulse on his neck, but I couldn't find one. "I don't think he's breathing."

"What do you mean?"

"I mean, I think he's dead."

Eleanor gasped. "Go find my aunt. I'm going to call for an ambulance and the sheriff." Eleanor nodded and did just that while I made the phone calls.

"Oh, hi, Angelica. How's it going?" said Dottie, the relatively new secretary at the sheriff's department. Seeing we were a small town, we didn't have a central dispatch. If you had a fire, you called the fire department. If you needed the sheriff, you called the sheriff's department.

"Hi, Dottie. Sorry, this is an emergency. I think one of our guests passed away at the inn. Can you send a deputy?"

"Someone died? How awful! Are you sure they're dead?" The receptionist sounded more curious than anything.

"I think so. He's not breathing. There's no pulse. And he's nonresponsive. I have no idea what happened to him. Looks like he was drinking a coffee and then just passed away. He's facedown in his room."

"My word. You don't hear of that every day."

Tell me about it. "Can you let a deputy know?"

"Oh, right. I'm on it. I'll send someone right away."

"Thank you." I hung up with Dottie and took advantage of being in the room alone to survey the scene. Mr. Haggerty had a rough draft of his article on Silverlake on the desk in the corner. I quickly scanned the document. He didn't have a nice thing to say about anyplace. I snapped a few pictures of the article and then a picture of the spilled drink. I didn't take any pictures of Mr. Haggerty himself. I didn't need to be reminded of what he looked like. The images would stay with me forever unless I used a memory charm to erase them.

I took a closer look at the coffee cup. It was the same cup that Diane served at the bakery. The heat was turned up in the room, and you could smell the pumpkin spice, but there was another scent under-lying it. I couldn't determine what it was, maybe black licorice? I wasn't sure if that was right or not. I wanted to take a closer look, but that was when Amber arrived, also known as Deputy Reynolds; although, I couldn't remember the last time I'd addressed her as such. She had a new deputy with her, one whom I hadn't been introduced to yet.

"What are you doing?" Amber said when she walked in. I still had my phone out. "Nothing. I just had a text message. I was waiting for you to arrive."

"Uh-huh." Amber looked over her shoulder at the new deputy and said, "Never trust what she says. She's always up to something."

"Hey," I started to interject but realized now wasn't the time. Amber bent low and checked Mr. Haggerty's vitals, concluding the same thing I had. There was no need to put a rush on the ambulance. Mr. Haggerty was dead.

The new deputy wasn't as interested in the body as she was in the rest of the room. Her instincts immediately went on alert as she began sniffing. "Do you smell that?" the new deputy asked.

"Smell what?" Amber took a cautionary sniff and scrunched her nose. "All I smell is pumpkin spice." Amber then turned to me. "Shifters," she rolled her eyes indicating that the new deputy was a shifter.

I ignored Amber and turned my attention to the new deputy, Deputy Lopez, according to her badge on her chest, and agreed with her. "No, I smell something too."

"What are you still doing in here? This is a crime scene, my crime scene, and you're stepping all over it," Amber snapped at me.

Aunt Thelma arrived on the scene just then. "What's going on here? Oh my word, is that Mr. Haggerty?"

"I'm afraid so. He must've passed away some-time between last night and today," I replied.

Amber stood up and walked toward us. "You seem pretty confident in that timeline of yours. Something else you're not telling us?"

I pointed down to the spilled latte. "Mr. Haggerty was at the high school last night, and Diane was selling pumpkin spice lattes." I meant the connection as just a time reference and not to implicate Diane in the crime. That's not the way Amber took it.

"Let's get an APB out on Diane Granger. Middle-aged woman. Chin-length brown hair. About five two."

Deputy Lopez nodded her head and was ready to spring into action when I spoke up. "No, hang on just a second. By all means, go and talk to Diane, but use common sense for once. Why would Diane kill Mr. Haggerty and ruin her reputation in the process? Diane would never do anything to jeopardize her business."

Aunt Thelma backed me up. "Angelica's right. You're always jumping to conclusions, Deputy Amber, and they're rarely correct."

Amber scoffed. "You don't know what you're talking about. My conviction record would say otherwise." Amber then turned back to Deputy Lopez. "Put the APB out. I'll stay here and secure the crime scene. On second thought, I'll call my father directly. It'll be faster."

Aunt Thelma and I excused ourselves from the room, and I immediately called Diane from my cell phone. Thankfully, Diane answered right away. "Hey, I have some bad news. Mr. Haggerty was just found dead in his hotel room."

"My goodness. That's awful. He was a horrible person, but now he's dead? I'm so sorry that you are dealing with that."

"That's not the worst of it. He had a pumpkin spice latte in his hand, and Amber's sending the sheriff to come question you." I hoped he was only going to question Diane. He certainly didn't have enough to arrest her. "I think you need to lawyer up."

Diane blew out a breath. "This is ridiculous, but you're right. Let me give Roger a quick call, and then do you know where Vance is?"

I looked at the clock on the wall above my head. "He's probably just finishing up with his run. I'll text him to call you right away."

Chapter 6

"Hey, are you okay?" Vance called me not more than five minutes later.

"Yeah, I'm okay. Did you talk to Diane?"

"I'm on my way to meet her now. I told her not to say anything to the sheriff until I could get there. What happened exactly?"

"There isn't much to tell. When Mr. Haggerty hadn't checked out, Eleanor asked me to stop by his room and get a move on things. When he didn't answer the door, Eleanor slipped inside and found him on the floor. I got inside as soon as I could and did a quick check of his vitals before calling it in."

"Did anything jump out at you that might help the case?"

I twisted my lips while I thought. "Just the coffee cup. Mr. Haggerty still had it in his hand. I pointed that out to Amber to try and help pinpoint the time of death, but she took it the wrong way." I was having some major guilt about that.

"No signs of a struggle?"

I mentally visualized the room. "I don't think so. Nothing was broken. The lamps and remotes were in place. The bed was even made, and now that I think about it, his luggage was packed. There weren't any dirty clothes on the floor other than some towels in the bathroom."

"Okay, so maybe our Mr. Haggerty died of natural causes."

"That's what I'm hoping. The room did smell off at first. It was hard to pick it up over the scent of pumpkin spice. Amber has a new deputy with her, Deputy Lopez. She's a shifter and picked up on it too. Dr. Humphrey's examining the body now, and I wonder what he thinks." Dr. Humphrey was a werewolf shifter and our town's medical examiner.

"It sounds like Amber is jumping the gun as usual," Vance remarked. I could hear his blinker clicking in the background.

"Aunt Thelma and I tried to tell her the same thing, but she blew us off. Tell Diane I'm really sorry. I wish I had kept my mouth shut about the coffee cup. I don't know what I was thinking."

"You were thinking that it would help to establish the time of death and nothing else. Don't worry. I'll tell the sheriff that he needs to determine the cause of death before he goes around questioning suspects."

"Okay, call me when you're done, and we can meet up."

"Sounds good. Love you."

"Love you too."

I hung up with Vance and attempted to have some semblance of normalcy around the inn. But, of course, news of a guest's death quickly circulated.

"Is it true someone died?" Jane came down and asked me without preamble.

"Yes, unfortunately."

"How?" Jane clutched her shawl close at her neck and peered cautiously down the hall toward Mr. Haggerty's room. "Are we safe here?" I could see the wheels inside Jane's head turning. She was already questioning their move to Silverlake.

"Oh, very much so." I tried to be as reassuring as possible. "I'm sure it was natural causes. It must have been his time."

We heard the door shut at the end of the hall, and then Dr. Humphrey's voice filled the small space. "Right there's your murder weapon. It was hard to smell the poison underneath all that pumpkin spice, but sure enough, it's there. Your deputy has a right fine sniffer on her." He turned in time to see Deputy Lopez smile. Amber didn't return the expression.

"Murder weapon?" Jane looked at me with horror.

"If you will excuse me for a moment, I'll be right back." I walked swiftly around the corner to catch Dr. Humphrey in the parking lot. The county staff was getting ready to remove Mr. Haggerty. I turned my attention from the gurney to the doctor.

"Dr. Humphrey?" I said, trying to stop him.

He turned and waited for me to catch up. Thankfully, Amber and Deputy Lopez kept walking.

"Can you make sure your guys take Mr. Haggerty out the side door here? I don't want to upset the guests more than they already are."

"Sure thing, Ms. Nightingale." Dr. Humphrey turned his attention toward the two workers with the gurney. "Harvey, Michelle, use the side exit, please," Dr. Humphrey instructed.

Dr. Humphrey turned to leave, but I stopped him with my words. "It was the coffee, then?"

Dr. Humphrey frowned. "I shouldn't have said that in the hallway."

"But you know you can trust me. Amber already thinks Diane's the killer, and you and I both know that's not true. If you were her friend, what would you do?"

"I'd hire her a good lawyer."

"Vance is already on his way to meet her. And then?"

Dr. Humphrey looked off into the distance.

"I'd be looking into Mr. Haggerty's background and see who would want him dead. Mind you, that's not professional advice. As a doctor, I should be telling you to avoid all dangerous situations and not put yourself in harm's way."

"Right, I know that. Don't worry. I'm not investigating this on my own." I wasn't sure if that made the doctor feel better or not. Instead, I changed the subject. "Do you know what poison was used?"

Dr. Humphrey nodded. "I have some ideas, but none that I'm ready to share."

Share with me was what he meant. I was almost positive the doctor knew what poison was used.

Again, the doctor turned to leave.

"It was the black licorice scent I smelled, wasn't it?" I replied to his back.

Dr. Humphrey looked over his shoulder. "I guess those feline instincts are stronger in you than I thought."

I never thought of myself as a true shifter. My gift to transform into a cat was a witch trait passed down from my mother's side. It required my amulet and a spell. My firstborn would inherit the gift as well. But Dr. Humphrey was right. I did have catlike instincts that extended past my love for naps and basking in the sun. Hopefully, it also meant I had nine lives, although I might be on life three or four by now.

Chapter 7

I called Vance and updated him with the news. It wasn't a good turn of events. It meant that we had to work smarter and faster to clear Diane's name and her business.

I shouldn't have been surprised when my phone rang thirty seconds after hanging up with Vance, and it was Clemmie.

"I've already put the tea on. Get down to the shop as soon as possible. We've got some sleuthing to do."

"Is Roger there?" I wondered how Diane's husband was holding up.

"Oh, he's here all right, and he's a wreck. I might have to slip some fire whiskey in his tea to help settle his nerves, or maybe I'll blast him with a spell or two instead. Hmmm." Clemmie seemed to think on it.

"Clemmie! You can't go around spelling your friends." I then thought of something. "You've never spelled me and not told me about it, have you?"

Clemmie was silent for a moment before she said, "Are you on your way here or not?"

"Clemmie! I can't believe you. When?"

"When what?"

"When did you spell me?"

"Which time?"

"Oh, my word. What do you mean? There's more than one time?"

"Perhaps. You can be a bit stubborn sometimes." Clemmie was unapologetic.

"You're trouble, do you know that?"

"As a matter of fact, I do. Are you coming down here then?"

"Let me talk with Aunt Thelma and make sure she's good with it. One of us has to stay at the inn today. It's going to be a mess." And hopefully not be a mass exodus once everyone finds out Mr. Haggerty was murdered. I felt torn. I wanted to stay and help my aunt, but I also wanted to help clear Diane.

Aunt Thelma popped her head out of the inn's front glass door. I was still on the phone with Clemmie. "Are you leaving or what? Clemmie says you better get a move on." Aunt Thelma held up her phone. I couldn't read the screen, but I assumed Clemmie had texted her.

"You sure?"

"Must I remind you that I ran this inn for thirteen years while you were off gallivanting around Chicago?"

"I wasn't gallivanting." I'd managed to build a successful career as a corporate event planner. By the look on my aunt's face, that was irrelevant. I shook my head. "You're right. I'm sorry." Aunt Thelma tossed me the keys to her Buick. "Call me if you change your mind. I'll come right back." Because even though Aunt Thelma had managed the inn while I was in Chicago, she also almost managed to run it into the ground. I couldn't think about that now. I turned my attention back to the phone. "Clemmie? I'll be there in a couple of minutes."

NORMALLY, when I wasn't in a hurry, I would've chosen to walk the Enchanted Trail to the Village Square shops. The wooded path circled the lake, and it was an excellent spot to clear your thoughts and center yourself. But today, time was of the essence.

Misty, Luke, and Roger were waiting for me when I walked into the tea shop. Clemmie motioned us to the back corner. She had put a dry-erase board up and had written the word "suspects" on the top of it. Clemmie's tea shop, Sit For a Spell, had two sides. One served as a retail space, and Clemmie used the other as a seating area. Patrons could take their tea and goodies, supplied by Diane's bakery, and sit at one of the tables or order full tea service.

Right now, all that was on hold as Clemmie locked the door and flipped the sign over to closed. "We have to make this quick. I have the Parson bridal party coming in at two," she said.

We all took a seat and faced the board.

"The sheriff's department has zeroed in on Diane, which we all know is rubbish," Clemmie continued.

I raised my hand and started to speak, not waiting for Clemmie to call on me. "That's because Mr. Haggerty had one of her pumpkin spice lattes in his hand when he died."

"That's just circumstantial evidence. We don't even know what the man died of!" Roger raised his voice.

"Unfortunately, we do." All eyes swiveled in my direction. "I overheard Dr. Humphrey at the inn. The latte was poisoned. I think he knows with what, but didn't tell me." Everyone took a moment to let that information sink in.

Misty spoke up first. "Even if the latte was poisoned and Diane sold it, that doesn't mean she's the one that poisoned the drink. Dozens, maybe even hundreds of people, picked up coffee from her last night, and no one else died. I know I had a pumpkin spice latte, and Mayor Parrish picked up a coffee. It was a chilly night."

"I know. Vance and I grabbed a coffee from her, and we're fine."

"Diane was set up," Luke stated.

"That's what I'm saying," Clemmie said.

"My wife didn't kill anyone," Roger said to no one in particular.

"We wouldn't be here if we thought she did. The question is, who did?" Clemmie asked.

"Good questions. Didn't Mr. Haggerty run his mouth at the tavern on Thursday night?" Misty asked.

"That's right. I was there. He was talking about how backward our town is and how he couldn't believe his editor sent him here in the first place." Luke folded his arms across his chest in frustration.

I took out my cell phone. "I snapped pics of the article Mr. Haggerty wrote. There was a draft of it on his desk." I brought up the pictures on my phone and enlarged the photo to read. "Let's see. He goes after me saying the Mystic Inn in Silverlake is three stars at best. You're better off saving your money and staying off-site an hour north in Atlanta." I skimmed ahead. "Some people might like ghosts waiting on them, but this author's opinion is they are best kept in the graveyard." I scowled in spite of myself at Mr. Haggerty's dig on Percy and Eleanor.

"Three stars? He doesn't know what he's talking about!" Clemmie exclaimed.

I smiled at my friend. "Don't worry. He insults everyone. Listen to this: If you wind up sick, you might be out of luck. There's a new healer in town, but rumor has it she's yet to prove herself. Your best to stay clear of her concoctions."

"Cassidy?" Misty asked.

"Yeah, I think that's who he means. He goes on to say: If you'd prefer a real doctor, Silverlake has a shifter that's rumored to be decent, if that's your thing. Just hope you don't have a real medical emergency. The community hospital leaves much to be desired."

"He did not say that," Clemmie seemed shocked.

I continued to scan the article. "He insults Craig and Bonnie at the tavern, Lacy at the charm shop, and Honor's candle shop. It goes on. Misty, he says you wouldn't know a bestseller even if you wrote it. Luke, he says your candy tastes stale." I looked up and met my friend's eyes.

"Stale? There isn't anything in my shop older than two days."

"Your chocolates are great," Roger said.

"Trust me, they are." I could eat a pound of Luke's fudge and still want more.

"What else did he say?" Misty asked.

I looked back at my phone. "He ends by saying:

The only bright spot this week provided a reminder of where not to go on vacation. If you like mediocrity in all things from accommodations, to food, to entertainment—then Silverlake is your place. As for me, I won't be returning anytime soon."

"I'd say good riddance, but it seems wrong seeing the man's dead," Misty said.

"I'll say it," Clemmie replied. "Good riddance."

"I agree. He insulted every member of this community with that article." Roger huffed.

"Right, but I'm not sure who else had a chance to read this. I'm going to bet one or two people, if any." It wasn't like Mr. Haggerty carried a draft of the article around with him.

"No, but he didn't hide his disdain. He said nasty comments to anyone," Misty added.

"He had no problem telling me tea was for old witches and vitamin-infused drinks were the way of the future." Clemmie rolled her eyes.

"Plus the tavern outburst," Luke reminded us.

"You're right. Even as I think back to last night, he got into it with Mayor Parrish a bit, insulting Terry Dawes." Luke raised his eyebrows. "I guess meat on a stick was the final straw," I answered his unspoken question.

"I thought that was brilliant. The twins loved it," Luke said.

"That's what Mayor Parrish said. But that only

led Mr. Haggerty to start insulting shifters and every other supernatural who's not a witch."

"Did Terry overhear what Mr. Haggerty said?" Luke asked.

"I don't know, possibly?" I replied.

"Terry's a grizzly shifter. You would think that if it was him, he would've snapped Mr. Haggerty's neck," Roger speculated.

"Unless he tried to make it look like it was someone else," Clemmic countered.

"I don't know about you, but I don't know Terry Dawes that well. Maybe we should look into him?" Misty suggested.

"You guys make some good points. We know none of us killed Mr. Haggerty even though he insulted our businesses. But we don't know Terry and I don't really know Cassidy that well, either." I felt like I knew most of the shop owners a bit better, but even they couldn't all be in the clear.

"Cassidy seems like a nice woman. We talked shop a time or two. She uses quite a bit of flowers in her medicines. But I agree, we don't know her well enough," Roger added.

"Here's what I'm thinking. I want to see if we can trace Mr. Haggerty's last twenty-four hours. Find out who he talked to and most likely insulted," I said.

"I can do that," Misty shot her hand up in the

air. "I'm trying to get my mind off things anyway," Misty grumbled to herself.

I let that last comment go. "Okay, while Misty does that, Roger, do you want to head to the bakery and check in with Diane about the kitchen? Hopefully, she's still there, and the sheriff doesn't have a search warrant yet. I think we should check the bakery's kitchen and make sure she's not been set up."

Roger nodded in agreement.

"Luke, do you want to look into Terry? See if you can find out where he was last night after he finished up at the high school?"

"You want an alibi," Luke replied.

"If possible. But try to keep it casual so they don't suspect anything," I replied.

"Okay, I'm on it."

"While you guys do that, I'm going to visit Connie and tell her about the latte. Maybe she has some idea what type of poison was used."

"Maybe we'll get double lucky, and Connie recently sold the ingredients," Clemmie pointed out.

"Yes, that would be helpful," I agreed.

"What do you want me to do?" Clemmie asked.

"Do what you do best. Listen to what people are saying, and see if you pick up any gossip." The tea shop would be bustling this afternoon. With a fresh murder on everyone's mind, they were sure to be talking about it.

"Put my ears on. You got it. I'll text you anything I hear."

"Great, I appreciate it." I looked around the group. "Any questions?"

"Nope, let's do this," Misty replied.

"Okay, great. Let's all catch up at the gala tonight. Sound good?"

There was a round of approvals, and then we all set out on our missions. "Misty, wait." My best friend had beelined it for the door.

"What? I thought you said time was of the essence."

"It is. I just wanted to check in with you after last night. Did you get a chance to talk to Daniel?"

"No, why bother? You heard what that psychic said. He's just going to break my heart."

"You cannot be serious," I kept my voice low.

"Listen, can we talk about this later? I only have a couple of hours, and I want to see how much I can piece together from last night."

I took a step back. "Yeah, absolutely." I left it at that, even though I wanted to tell my best friend to stop being ridiculous. I knew my well-meaning comment would only backfire.

Chapter 8

Connie's shop, Mix it Up! was also located in Village Square. It was a quick power walk to the front of the shopping district to her shop's front door. I knew she would be busy, given it was a Saturday afternoon and the bicentennial celebration. What I hadn't expected was the line snaking out front. I had been hoping for a quick word, but it didn't look like that would happen. I bypassed the line and walked into the shop's adjoining door. It turned out people weren't waiting in line to enter the shop but rather for a free sample of whatever potion Connie was brewing. The entire shop smelled sweet, like apples. Connie stood behind the counter and used a ladle to fill a tray full of small cups a staff member held for her. As soon as it was full, the staff member turned and walked over to the visitors in line and began passing them out.

"My goodness, you're busy," I said from behind Connie. She looked over her shoulder. "My fall promotion turned out better than I could've ever imagined."

"What are you mixing up today?"

"It's an energy potion. A temporary restorative drought. It makes you feel like a million bucks, if only for a few hours. Want to try some?"

I looked at the long line standing before her.

"I don't want to cut."

Connie turned around one of the cups in her hand. "It's okay. I heard about your morning. You deserve this." Connie winked and handed the cup over.

The warmth of the potion seeped into my hands through the cup. I brought it to my lips and took a sip. It tasted surprisingly like hot apple cider. "This is really good."

"Wait until the magic kicks in. It'll be even better."

A moment later, I understood what Connie meant. Any traces of fatigue vanished, and I felt full of energy. Even my mood seemed to lighten, and I didn't think I had been that down to begin with. "I'm smiling. Why am I smiling?" I said with a laugh.

"You can't help smiling when you feel so good," Connie said as she filled up another tray. When she finished, she wiped her hand off on a towel and then turned to give me her full attention.

"Okay, I have two minutes. What can I do for you?"

It took me a moment to remember why I had stopped to talk with her in the first place. Her feel-good potion was that strong. I crossed my fingers that the effects would wear off a bit so I could focus on the case.

I got my thoughts in order and relayed the morning's events and Dr. Humphrey's suspicion about the poison.

"What did you say it smelled like?" Connie asked.

"I want to say black licorice?"

"Do you have a sample of it by chance?"

"I don't. Some did spill on the carpet. I also took some pictures." I took out my phone and brought up the picture, zooming in toward the spill. I hadn't examined it that well in person, and on the phone, it was almost impossible to tell the difference between the potion and a regular pumpkin spice latte.

"I don't know. It could be a couple of things. Sleep of the Dead can have a spicy scent. And you know if you take enough of it, it will kill you." I knew what Sleep of the Dead was. The community hospital used it for anesthesia. Connie was the local supplier. She made it in larger batches and supplied it to the hospital. You had to be careful if you stopped in while she was making it. If you took too big of a whiff, you'd pass out stone cold.

"Tell you what, how about I stop by after closing up and take a look at it? Would that work?"

"I think so." I wasn't sure if the room was still considered a crime scene and if we were allowed back in. I thought I'd better head back and find out. Not only that, but if we were allowed back in the room, I didn't want Eleanor to clean up the stain. "I'll call you if that doesn't work."

"Perfect. What time is it?"

"Almost three o'clock." I couldn't believe the hours were flying by. I had to start getting ready for the gala.

"Okay, I'll see you in a couple of hours then."

I said goodbye to Connie and hustled back to the inn. It turned out that Dr. Humphrey's team had photographed every square inch of the room, and Deputy Lopez was wrapping up collecting fingerprints and tagging Mr. Haggerty's belongings. Soon the team would be done gathering evidence and recording the scene, and they'd turn the room back over to us.

Surprisingly, or maybe not given Mr. Haggerty's reputation, no one was all that upset he had died, other than Jane, but she was more concerned for Amelia's safety. But even Jane seemed at ease after she realized it wasn't a random attack.

"No one checked out?" I asked my aunt.

"Just one room, and it had nothing to do with Mr. Haggerty. A nice older couple from Savannah. Their daughter went into labor a few weeks early. It turns out they're going to be grandparents for the first time."

"That's exciting."

"That's what I told them! Unfortunately, Amber insisted on searching them before left. After that, I'm not sure if they'll ever come back."

Our conversation was cut short by the arrival of Deputy Lopez and Eleanor.

"Did you want me to call in a cleaning crew?" the deputy offered. Eleanor looked offended. "No offense to your skills, ma'am," Deputy Lopez quickly clarified.

"I believe the deputy means as in a biohazard team." I looked to the deputy to back me up.

Deputy Lopez nodded. "It's standard procedure. The spilled coffee could be considered a biohazard."

I quickly jumped in. "Oh, no, no. We can manage the stain. Eleanor is brilliant at removing them." I may have been a bit overenthusiastic by the way Eleanor and Deputy Lopez looked at me. "I only mean that I'm sure you guys are busy, and we can handle the rest. But I appreciate the offer."

"Okay, let us wrap up here, and then we'll get out of your hair. In the meantime, call the station if you come across any evidence or hear of something we should know."

I wanted to ask Deputy Lopez if she meant that. She seemed like a nice person, but it was too soon to tell. So far, Deputy Jones was the nicest deputy in the department, and he mostly just humored me. Although, even he had to admit my hunches were often right.

Eleanor and I walked away from the deputy back toward the reception desk, where I motioned for Eleanor to follow me to the back office. I quietly shut the door behind us.

Aunt Thelma was already in the office. "What's going on, dear?"

I explained to my aunt and Eleanor about Connie coming over to examine the stain.

"That's why you didn't want the cleaning crew to come," Eleanor surmised.

"Exactly. Connie is brilliant with potions. I'm hoping she can figure out what it is, which will give us another clue and lead us to the killer." That was my plan anyway.

Chapter 9

I wasted no time getting ready, the entire time hoping to hear from Vance and see how things had gone with Diane and the sheriff. Thankfully, Vance texted me at five o'clock, saying he was wrapping up at the sheriff's department and he would come to pick me up after going home and freshening up.

I twisted my hair and pinned it with a faux diamond clip to match my earrings.

"You look beautiful," Aunt Thelma sighed as I clipped the second diamond earring on. The earrings belonged to my mother, and Aunt Thelma had kept them safe all these years.

"Thank you," I stepped back and smoothed the dark blue satin dress across my waist. "It's not too much?" I thought about using a bit of glamour on my face, but I didn't want to end up looking like I'd robbed a cosmetics counter, so I thought I better play it safe and do it old school with a bit of blush and mascara.

"Not at all. You'll be the belle of the ball if I do say so myself."

I looked over at my aunt, who seemed to have a tear in her eye. "What's wrong?"

"Oh, nothing. I'm just an old lady turning into a watering pot." Aunt Thelma waved her hand at her eyes and looked up at the ceiling to dry her tears.

"Stop it. You're not old." Not that anyone could ever guess her age. My aunt and Clemmie were both known to splash on age-defying potions every now and again. My aunt might be approaching retirement, but she didn't look a day over forty-five. Sooner or later, people were bound to think we were sisters.

"Your mother would be so proud if she could see you now." Aunt Thelma sniffled.

My aunt had stepped in and raised me when my mother passed away when I was a young girl, acting very much like a mother. I relayed the thought to my aunt. "You didn't have to give up your life and raise me, but you did. In so many ways, you are my mother, and I know she's smiling down on us from heaven. Thank you for being you."

"I do believe that's the nicest thing you've ever said to me. But you know, it was an honor to raise you. Except for the teenage years, oh and that time you ghosted me." Aunt Thelma winked. "Now excuse me while I grab a tissue. My makeup is running down my face." Aunt Thelma dabbed at the corner of her eyes with her fingertips.

"Knock, knock," Vance said as he opened the apartment's front door and stepped inside. He looked handsome as ever in a black suit and tie.

"Don't the two of you make a pretty picture," Aunt Thelma said, sniffling a bit.

Vance caught my eye. His expression seemed to question if everything was okay.

"It's okay. We were sharing a moment."

"Ah," Vance remarked.

"How is Diane holding up?" I asked.

"She's alright. Luckily for us, the sheriff and Amber didn't want to miss the gala any more than we did, and they didn't have enough to hold her. Not that they didn't try."

"They searched the bakery?"

"They did, and they ran into Roger there and tried to say he was destroying evidence, but the workers confirmed he got there two minutes before the sheriff did. Diane's cameras confirmed it."

"I didn't know she had cameras now," I remarked.

It was Aunt Thelma's turn to join in the conversation. "Oh, yes. She and Roger both installed them. I think maybe we should here, too." The security system was about the only thing we hadn't upgraded at Mystic Inn. After the old system quit working, we never bothered to replace it.

"The sheriff held Diane until he went through all the footage from Friday night but didn't come up with anything. Mr. Haggerty never even stepped foot in the bakery, and without any evidence from the kitchen, they couldn't keep her."

"But didn't Mr. Haggerty get the latte from the high school?" I asked.

"That's the assumption, but nobody has proof. Diane doesn't even remember waiting on him Friday night, so it must have been one of her workers."

"So there was a chance he could've gone into the bakery," Aunt Thelma thought out loud.

"That's what the sheriff wanted to rule out. That's also where Diane had prepared the drinks," Vance supplied.

I thought back to Friday night. Diane hadn't brought her barista equipment with her. Instead, she had brought prefilled stainless steel urns. The kind that held fifty cups of coffee. She kept them plugged in to keep the drinks hot.

"If dozens of people drank from the same coffee pot and nobody else got sick—"

"That means that the killer took advantage of Mr. Haggerty drinking coffee and slipped the potion into his drink when he wasn't looking. Or that's the angle we presented to the sheriff."

"So, it's someone who bumped into him last night after he grabbed a latte," I added.

"That only leaves almost everyone who lives in Silverlake. The high school was lit," Aunt Thelma remarked.

"Lit?" I looked at my aunt.

"You know, it was popping," Aunt Thelma did her best impersonation of a DJ spinning her tracks.

Vance chuckled, amused at Aunt Thelma's use of slang.

I closed my eyes and shook my head. "Yes, the high school was busy last night. Anyway, does that mean the murder is premeditated?" I asked.

"How so?" Vance asked.

"Think about it. The murder weapon is a potion. Who goes around carrying a deadly potion if they don't plan on using it?"

"I've been known to carry one in my purse a time or two," Aunt Thelma chimed in.

"Let me rephrase that. What sane, rational witch goes around carrying a deadly potion?" I lovingly teased my aunt.

"I hadn't thought of that," Vance remarked.

"Our killer was waiting for the right opportunity," I said.

"And happened to find it Friday night," Vance concluded.

"Too bad we have no idea who he is." Aunt Thelma frowned.

I almost forgot that Connie was stopping by until there was another knock on the apartment door. "It's probably Connie. She said she was going to stop by and look at the stain," I explained to Vance as I walked over to answer the door.

Vance picked up my train of thought, "Maybe she can identify the potion."

"That's what I'm hoping."

Five minutes later, we were at the scene of the crime. Even with the stain on the carpet, you would never have known a man died there hours before. Unfortunately, with all the traffic in and out of the room, I could no longer smell the particular scent that had intrigued me this morning.

"It looks like a regularly spilled cup of coffee," Connie remarked, keeping a short distance. "I don't see any metallic flaking, do you?"

"No, I don't think so, but I haven't looked too close," I remarked. Vance and Aunt Thelma agreed.

"Do you mind?" Connie asked, motioning to the bedside lamp.

"No, be my guest. Do whatever you think is best," I explained.

Connie unplugged the lamp, took it toward the stain, and plugged it in to a nearby outlet. Unfortunately, even under the added light, the stain looked rather ordinary. "That's disappointing," Connie remarked.

I frowned, not because she was wrong, but because I tended to agree.

"Sleep of the Dead reflects bits of gold under the right light, but this potion is flat as can be."

I twisted my lips and looked over to Vance. He reached over and wrapped his arm around my shoulder in a comforting gesture.

"I guess it's a good thing I brought my special equipment." I looked around the room. Connie was dressed in a black sequin cocktail dress. I wasn't sure where she kept her specialized equipment, but it wasn't in her dress. Connie walked over to the dresser and opened her clutch purse, retrieving a small flashlight. The metal tube was about four inches long. Connie pushed a button, and the light portion popped out of the end, doubling the piece's length. Connie moved to close the blackout curtain and block out the setting sun. "Hit the lights, will you?" Vance nodded and did just that. I wasn't sure what Connie was doing until she turned on the flashlight, and I realized it wasn't just a regular bulb but a black light. The moment the beams came in contact with the carpet, the stain began to glow bright red.

"It's your lucky day. Well, so to speak." Connie stood up and motioned for Vance to turn on the light. We all blinked as our eyes readjusted to the brightness. "There's loxie in the stain."

"Loxie?" I replied.

"The killer probably used a Final Night potion. There was a famous case in London in the 1920s. A woman used it to kill four different husbands after they each accused her of being a witch."

"She sort of proved their point, didn't she?" Vance questioned.

"That she did. Unfortunately for her, one of the detectives was a witch, and he put the case together after smelling black licorice at the crime scenes."

"Is it a hard potion to make?" Aunt Thelma asked

"It's not complicated except for the final ingredient—a midnight orchid. It can be tricky to find."

"It's a black orchid, right?" Suddenly, the case was starting to come together.

"It is. Why? Have you seen one?" Connie asked.

"The centerpieces for tonight's gala. Each one has a black orchid in the middle. I wonder if it's the same flower?"

"We better get to the gala and find out. Roger should be there." Aunt Thelma moved toward the door.

"Let's get going then," I said. "The sooner we talk to Roger, the better."

———————————

Chapter 10

———————————

The night sky was aglow with the bright lights shining from the city hall. The streets were filled with people dressed in their finest attire, making their way to the entrance. The sounds of laughter and chatter filled the air as guests made their way up the red carpet, which was lined with velvet ropes. The outside of the building was adorned with colorful banners that added to the festive atmosphere. The entrance was guarded by smartly dressed security personnel who checked the guests' invites before letting them through. As the guests made their way inside, they were greeted by the sounds of a live band playing soft music and the warm glow of candlelight. The gala promised to be a night to remember.

We couldn't find Diane and Roger, but we found Misty and Luke.

"Hey, what did you guys find out today?" Misty asked when we joined them. She could tell I was on a mission.

"We think we know what potion was used to poison Mr. Haggerty. Have you seen Roger?"

"I don't think he's here yet." Luke scanned the crowd.

"I haven't seen Diane yet, either," Misty confirmed.

"Let me know as soon as you see them in case we're not together. I have my phone on me." I shot off a quick text to Diane, asking if they were on their way, while Vance explained the flower connection.

"Did you find out anything about Terry?" I asked Luke while putting my phone back in my purse.

"Only that he doesn't like me."

"How so?" I asked.

"I don't know. I guess I'm not very good at this detective business. I thought it would be best to run into him casually, so I followed him to the hardware store, but he saw right through me. Newsflash: don't try and stalk a grizzly. He chewed me out on the spot and wanted to know what I had against shifters. He threatened to take it outside."

"That could be promising," Misty remarked.

Luke looked taken aback.

I bobbed my head from side to side. "Misty

might be right. The fact Terry jumped on the defense could mean he's hiding something."

"What are you guys all chatting about? Better not be that awful journalist's death," Mayor Parrish said, joining our circle.

None of us could hide our guilty expressions.

Clemmie didn't even try. "You mean his murder."

Mayor Parrish balked. "Murder? You must be mistaken. That can't be. I thought he must've passed from natural causes."

"Not unless he poisoned himself," Aunt Thelma revealed.

Mayor Parrish kept her voice low. "Does anyone else know about this?"

"What? That he was poisoned?" Aunt Thelma asked. The mayor nodded. "A few people, but what do you expect? You can't sweep murder under the rug."

Mayor Parrish looked both ways to see if anyone was eavesdropping. "I'm only thinking of the town. I don't want Mr. Haggerty's death marring this historic event."

"That will never happen. Mr. Haggerty's death isn't going to define our community," I said with more feeling than I meant to.

"If that's the case, then disperse, all of you, and make merry. We have a sapphire to reveal." Mayor

Parrish shooed us, forcing us to break up our group and table our conversation.

Five minutes later, Mayor Parish stood at the center of the stage. The crowd hushed to listen to her speech, "Ladies and Gentlemen of Silverlake, it is with great pride and humility that I stand before you tonight to reveal the heart and soul of our town — the Silverlake Sapphire. For generations, this precious gemstone has been the source of our town's enchantment and has given us the power to thrive and flourish. As we gather here tonight to celebrate our town's rich history and prosperous future, let us never forget the true essence of what makes Silverlake so special. So without further ado, it is my pleasure to present to you…" The mayor nodded to the hired guards standing behind her. They moved into position, standing beside the silk-draped pedestal and looking like Christmas toy soldiers with their red uniforms, shiny gold buttons, and black bearskin hats. With all the pomp and circumstance, they seemed more for show than anything else. "The Silverlake Sapphire!" On cue, a guard lifted the fabric and whisked it away dramatically.

A gasp ripped through the crowd.

The case was empty.

"I told you this would happen! The magic will be ruined and on the town's bicentennial!" I recognized the shout from council member Vera O'Malley. She'd expressed her concerns about revealing the sapphire after being voted on the council after Mr. Craddock's death this summer.

The flashing lights from the townspeople's cameras added to the frenzy, making it feel like a chaotic scene from a movie premiere.

Mayor Parrish raised her voice. "I'm sure it's around here somewhere. Perhaps we simply forgot to bring it out?" Mayor Parrish looked around the audience for a lifeline. The crowd was talking amongst themselves, clearly confused and concerned about the missing sapphire. They were throwing theories out left and right. Mayor Parrish had to work fast to reign them in. She clapped her hands and drew the attention back to herself. "We'll come back to the sapphire. For now, let's cut the cake, shall we?" Mayor Parrish excused herself and headed straight for me. "Find that sapphire," she hissed before turning and plastering on a fake smile. "This way, everyone. Wait until you see the cake!"

I caught Misty's eye and motioned with my head to meet me down the hall. Luke was still beside her, and he followed along. Aunt Thelma and Clemmie tracked us and joined in too. We rendezvoused in the mayor's office.

"This is rotten luck," Misty flopped down in the mayor's plush office chair.

"I'm going to round up the council members

and see what they want to do. See if we can do anything," Aunt Thelma said.

"Okay, while you do that, we'll see if we can find the sapphire," I said.

"Let's use magic. If the sapphire's here, we'll find it," Vance suggested.

"Summoning charms?" Misty suggested.

"Good idea. We can split up. I'll head to the coat check area." It might be too easy, but I didn't want to overlook the obvious hiding places.

"I'll check with the catering company," Vance proposed.

"I'll head downstairs to the storage rooms," Luke offered.

"I'll go with you. We can check the county clerk's office on the way," Misty suggested.

"I'm going to go eavesdrop and see what I can learn," Clemmie added.

I took a deep breath. City hall was more than just a ballroom. It was a working government building. Searching the space in its entirety was going to take some time.

When I got to the coat check room, I realized I wasn't alone.

Amelia was in the coat check crying. Beatrice and Sabrina were there trying to bring her comfort. "This is not your fault," Beatrice said.

"It's not like you stole the sapphire," Sabrina added.

"I hate that my prediction came true, though. I told the mayor I had a bad feeling about it. I told her someone might try to steal it."

"Then it's definitely not your fault." Beatrice shook her head.

"Yeah, the mayor should've listened to you. If it's anyone's fault, it's hers," Sabrina said.

"Totally," Beatrice agreed.

But Amelia didn't listen. "This is all my fault," she continued to sob.

I cleared my throat to announce my presence. "Hey, listen to the girls. The only person responsible is the person who stole it. You did the right thing by telling us you were worried about it. If anything, we owe you an apology for not taking your warning seriously."

Amelia continued to sniffle.

"There you are," Jane said with relief. "Oh, don't cry." Jane rushed forward and hugged her daughter, rubbing her back. "I know you feel bad, but how many times do I have to tell you it's not your fault. You can only see the future. It's up to other people to change it."

"I know. I just wish they'd listen," Amelia said to her mother's chest.

"I know. So do I," Jane agreed.

"Is there any way you can see who has it?" Beatrice asked.

Amelia wiped at her eyes. "I wish I could. I can't

usually control what I see. But I could try." Amelia looked hopefully up at her mother.

"How about in a little bit when you're not so upset?" Jane suggested. "I don't want you to overdo it."

Amelia hiccupped as she fought to control her crying. "That would probably be best," she managed to say.

"Come on, honey. I think we should get going." Jane took her daughter's hand.

"Okay, mom," Amelia agreed.

"We'll see you all later." Jane offered a sad smile, and the two headed for the doors.

"That's a real bummer," Sabrina said.

"I know. I really like Amelia. I wish she weren't so sad," Beatrice bit her bottom lip before an idea seemed to strike her. "Wait a minute, what if you find the sapphire?" She pointed at me.

"That's a great idea," her sister agreed. "You're so great at finding stuff. Look at all those other mysteries you solved. This here should be a piece of cake, right?"

"That was actually what I was trying to do. My friends and I are trying summoning charms to see if we can locate the sapphire." I walked toward the ballroom's entrance and scanned the guests. The twins followed me.

"Ooooh, we know how to do summoning charms. Can we try too?" Beatrice asked.

"I don't see why not. Do you know what the sapphire looks like?"

"Uh-huh. We saw it in the history book, remember?" Beatrice said to Sabrina.

"But just to refresh our memory, maybe you could tell us the spell again?" Sabrina asked.

I smiled. "When you want to do a summoning charm, the magic words are Éla edó. Remember, it's important to picture the object you're searching for. The closer you are to getting the image right, the better the chance of the spell working. Do you want to try it?" The girls nodded enthusiastically. I expected them to run off and fetch their wands, perhaps from even their coat pockets, but instead, they surprised me by withdrawing them from up their sleeves. I suppose I shouldn't be surprised by anything the twins did. If anything, they were always prepared.

"Now close your eyes and picture the sapphire. On the count of three, raise your wand, and we'll say the spell together." I copied the instructions as I relayed them. With my eyes closed, I said, "One, two, three: Éla edó." I felt the magic burst from my wand and shoot out into the ballroom.

Shrieks and gasps followed as jewelry soared through the air toward us. Necklaces raced past people's faces while earrings popped free and bracelets flew off of people's wrists and sailed in our direction. People screamed and grasped for their belongings, but the spell was too powerful.

The girls and I held out our hands to protect our faces as bracelets, rings, and earrings pelted us.

"Tixie!" I shouted, trying to stop the spell, but for once, it wasn't my magic that had caused the chaos. "Stop the spell!" I shouted to the girls as more jewelry continued to assault us.

"Adios!" Beatrice shouted.

Sabrina copied her and repeated the spell. It was a reverse spell and not the one I would've chosen at that moment. The jewelry that had hit the floor rose back into the air and sailed across the room, attempting to reunite with its owners.

The sound of metal clanking against metal and the sharp impact of pieces hitting walls filled the air. The magical energy was palpable, crackling in the air like electricity. More shouts and hollers followed as people either ducked for cover or attempted to retrieve their belongings, bumping into one another.

Mayor Parrish dashed around the corner as fast as her petite legs could carry her. "What in the world is happening?" she asked as she clutched her pearls. The strand was no longer around her neck but held tightly in her fist.

"We were trying to summon the sapphire," I explained.

"With what spell?" Mayor Parrish replied with exasperation.

"Angelica was teaching us a summoning charm, but I guess Sabrina and I don't really remember what the sapphire looks like after all." Beatrice looked sheepish.

"It's green, right?" Sabrina asked.

"No, silly, that's an emerald," Beatrice rolled her eyes.

"Oh, sorry." Sabrina looked apologetic.

"It's purple!" Beatrice replied confidently with the tone of an older sister (even if it was only by two minutes.)

The mayor frowned at our trio, and I suddenly felt as if I were a child again.

I stepped up. "Don't worry. We'll make sure everyone gets their jewelry back."

"I'm not worried about everyone's jewelry. Just find the sapphire!"

"Right, we're on it!" Beatrice beamed.

"Never fear. We're on the case!" Sabrina saluted the mayor, and I turned away to keep from smiling. You had to love the twins' enthusiasm, even when things turned into a disaster.

It took a little bit, but eventually, everyone had all their valuables back. Unfortunately, we never did find the town's sapphire. We ended up regrouping in Mayor Parrish's office for a powwow while the twins continued the hunt.

Aunt Thelma had left. The town council members held an emergency meeting and decided to guard the town's magical borders with backup charms that would alert them if someone crossed the border on foot. The main enchantments were still intact, which meant the stone was still in Silverlake, but who knew how long it would be? Council members were also stationed at the town's main entrance, and they planned on searching every car as it passed through. They were currently debating what spells to use. It was a daunting prospect and not very practical seeing how many visitors were in town.

We needed to find the sapphire.

All of us turned our heads when Diane arrived. "Why is the mayor telling me to come back here?"

"Someone stole the sapphire," Misty replied.

"Are you kidding me? And I thought I had a rough day."

Misty gave Diane a quick rundown of everything that had happened.

"Is Roger with you?" I knew we were supposed to be finding the sapphire, but right then, I wanted to ask him about the orchid.

"What do you mean? He's not here? He told me he would organize the shop after delivering the last centerpiece and then meet me here, but that was hours ago. Let me try his cell phone."

Diane walked off and attempted to reach Roger. But she had no luck. "I hope he's okay."

"What about the cameras? Can you check them from your phone?" Vance asked.

"I forgot about that," I spoke up.

"Diane showed me the app earlier," Vance explained.

"But I can never get it to work. Can you try?" Diane walked toward me with her phone. "I swear, technology and I don't mix." Diane handed me her phone and pointed to the security app.

I pushed the button to launch the program and then handed Diane the phone to enter her credentials. "I'm not sure what I'm supposed to do after that. It's too complicated," Diane confessed.

I had to smile because while there were a lot of options to choose from, the one that stood out the most was the big red button that said live stream. "I think if you click on this, it'll show you the current cameras." I clicked the button to see what would happen, and as soon as the video loaded, Diane and I screamed.

The live stream showed the florist's shop in a raging inferno. The roof was ablaze, with flames licking at the sky and smoke billowing out of the windows.

"What's wrong?" Misty rushed forward.

Diane and I couldn't move fast enough. We were trying to walk out the door and speak simultaneously. "There's a fire at the florist!" I managed to say. I couldn't help that I was yelling. "We have to get there as fast as possible." I couldn't see Roger on the cameras, but what if he was trapped inside?

We all ran out of the mayor's office. Vance was the only one of us thinking. He called the fire department before we were even to the main ballroom. Clemmie did one better and sought out Fire Chief Grady from the crowd. Together, we all raced to Village Square with the firetrucks leading the way.

Chapter 11

"Is Roger okay?" Aunt Thelma asked as she arrived with Diane. Vance and I had left them at the car, and we raced it on foot once we got to Village Square, but it had been no use. Someone had spotted the fire before we did, and the trucks were already at the scene, blocking us from going any farther.

I shook my head because I didn't know. We weren't allowed anywhere near the fire and so far, we had only seen firefighters run toward the blaze, along with Luke. He was a volunteer firefighter.

A magical rain cloud soon appeared above Village Square and water began to pour down. Vance took off his suit coat and covered my shoulders with it. Together, we all sought shelter under one of the other shop's porches. Smoke blew through the air, and the rain continued to pound down. I prayed that the fire would be contained and that Roger was safe. The alternative was too horrible to bear.

Just then, an ambulance pulled into the parking lot. The EMTs jumped out and were on the move, running through the cobblestone streets directly toward Roger's shop. The suspense was killing us, and it only got worse when a second ambulance arrived. We didn't dare ask any questions. I think we were all afraid of what they might say. Instead, we stood there in silence. Aunt Thelma and Clemmie on either side of Diane, holding her up and giving her all their strength.

Diane cried softly, and I could understand her pain. The scene was chaotic, and I was becoming overwhelmed by it all. My mind was racing, trying to figure out what to do. I felt a surge of empathy for Diane and the situation we were all in. I hated feeling helpless.

It felt like ages, but eventually we saw Roger. Diane saw him first. The EMTs wheeled him out. The back of the bed had been elevated, and he had an oxygen mask over his face.

"Roger!" Diane said as she rushed forward. "Thank goodness you're all right!" Diane wept. You could tell she wanted to throw her arms around her husband, but she was afraid to.

"I'd be even better if my shop wasn't on fire and

I hadn't taken a beating to the back of the head." Roger closed his eyes in pain.

"Someone attacked you?" Diane said in shock.

"Ma'am, we really must keep moving. Your husband needs to go to the hospital," the EMT interrupted. It was still raining, and we were thoroughly drenched.

"Right, I'm sorry. I'm coming with you." The EMTs nodded, and the rest of us stood off to the side and let them pass through.

An odd mixture of relief and anger rolled through me. I was so grateful that Roger was safe and yet angered all the same that this had happened to him.

"Did you hear what he said? Someone attacked him," Clemmie said as we walked back to the overhang.

"That probably means it was a shifter. A witch would've just used a spell," Aunt Thelma whispered. "I hate sounding like that, but we have to look at the evidence."

"You do make a point," Clemmie agreed.

I wasn't sure what to think. The entire past twenty-four hours had my head scrambled and my emotions on overload.

For a long time, I felt rooted to the spot and watched the firefighters work. Roger was alive, but someone had tried to kill him, and they definitely had wanted to destroy his shop.

"You know it was Mr. Haggerty's killer, right? Who set the fire," I clarified.

Vance nodded. "They didn't want any evidence being traced back to them. They probably figured it was only a matter of time before someone made the orchid connection to the poison."

"Which means they got it from Roger's shop." Whether they purchase it or stole it was yet to be determined. "I know now's not the time, but I want to talk to Roger and see if he remembers selling orchids to anyone else. If the killer knows he can identify him—"

"He'd still be in danger," Vance finish the thought that I was unable to say out loud.

"I think we better call Deputy Jones and give them a heads-up." I know Deputy Lopez said to give her a call if anything came up, but I wasn't sure how I felt about her yet. I knew Deputy Jones would see to it.

"You're right."

Fire Chief Grady came back through the center of Village Square covered in soot and looking worse for the wear. The once meticulous courtyard was now trampled. Pumpkins had been rolled to the side and plants flattened by the pressure of the fire hose. A minor price to pay to save the rest of the shops.

I wasn't surprised to see the local news van pull in, and out popped reporter Kara Black. She was no Stormy Evans, and that was a good thing. It was never a good thing whenever *Witch News Network* rolled into town. The cameraman quickly got in position, and the duo was soon reporting live from the scene. Vance and I were sure to keep out of the way as we stood off to the side letting everything sink in.

"Chief Grady!" Kara shouted to get the fireman's attention. "Can you give us a quick update?"

The fire chief was talking to a couple of his men but nodded that he would join her in a moment.

"What can you tell us about the blaze?" Kara asked the moment he joined her.

"The fire's out, and we managed to contain it to the florist's shop. There's a bit of smoke damage to the charmery and cloak shop, but it should be minor."

Kara volleyed the microphone back and forth. "Do you know how it started?"

"We're still in the preliminary portion of this investigation. We should know more in the next day or two," Chief Grady replied.

"The damage looks like it's coming from the back," Kara pointed out.

"Yes, the fire was primarily in the back of the building. That's where we believe it was initiated."

"Initiated? Does this mean you know what caused the fire?"

"Again, we'll know more in a few days. If you'll

excuse me." The fire chief didn't wait to hear whatever else Kara was going to say.

"If it was in the back, the killer could've been trying to destroy the orchids," I said out loud while trying to picture the layout of Roger's shop. Like most of the village's shops, the front was retail space, and the back housed inventory and a small office. That gave me an idea. Chief Grady was finishing up with the reporter when I flagged him down.

"Hey, I know you're busy, but I just wanted to let you know that I think this fire ties in with Mr. Haggerty's death."

"The journalist?" Chief Grady asked.

"That's the one. He was poisoned, we think with a flower from Roger's shop. We know Roger has a camera system—"

"Had a camera system. The security system was ground zero from the blaze."

"Shoot. Okay, thanks." I turned to Vance after the chief walked away. "The killer was definitely destroying evidence." I sighed in frustration. We had to catch this person, and fast.

Chapter 12

The next morning as I lay in bed, I couldn't decide which case to tackle first. The reality of a killer roaming free in Silverlake, just waiting to strike again, was enough to send my anger spiking. But the thought of Silverlake losing its sapphire and all of its magical protection broke my heart. I reached out, grabbed my wand off the nightstand, and flicked my wrist to conjure my bathrobe. I would've summoned a cup of coffee, but that meant I would've robbed it from someone else, most likely Aunt Thelma, with how conjuring worked. You see, things didn't just appear out of thin air. They always came from somewhere else. It was one thing to conjure something you owned and another to conjure something you wanted, which meant I had to shuffle my feet to the kitchen to brew my morning cup of joe.

I was getting ready to do that when Vance texted me and asked about meeting up for breakfast. It sounded like an excellent idea to me, and we agreed to meet at the diner in thirty minutes. Now, you know I love Vance's mom's Montecristo sandwich. She has one even better at breakfast. It has French toast, honey ham, and loads of cheese. Pair that with a strong cup of coffee, and you were sure to be full until well past lunchtime. Breakfast couldn't come fast enough.

"Morning, Love," Vance stood and greeted me with a kiss on the cheek when I met him at the diner. He had already reserved us one of the side booths.

"There's my favorite soon-to-be daughter." Heather stopped by and served me a hot cup of coffee. "You doing okay?" Vance's mom had the biggest heart out of anyone I knew. I was lucky she was going to be my mother-in-law.

"I'm doing all right, thanks," I replied with a soft smile that didn't quite reach my eyes. I wouldn't feel like myself until everything was put to rights in Silverlake.

"The usual?" Heather referred to our orders.

"Yes, please," I replied.

"Thanks, mom," Vance added.

"I talked to Deputy Jones last night," Vance said as we doctored our coffees. "He agreed to have security guard Roger."

"That's good. Did he say how Roger's doing?"

"He didn't know much, but I thought we could head to the hospital after this?"

"Good idea. How about we have your mom put in a to-go order, and we can take it up there. If Diane's still there, she's probably starving."

"I'm sure she is. She said she wasn't going to leave his side when I saw her last."

"That sounds about right." Knowing Diane, she wouldn't even leave to slip down to the cafeteria for a quick bite.

Vance and I drank our coffees in companionable silence, both lost in our thoughts.

"I didn't tell you. He was here Friday night." Heather stopped by with a coffee pot. "Refill?" she offered.

I slid my cup forward for her to top it off. Vance did the same.

"Who?" he asked.

"That journalist, Mr. Haggerty."

I leaned forward. "Around what time?"

"About nine o'clock. I was going to close up early. We were pretty dead with everyone at the high school, but then he came in."

"Did you talk with him?" Vance asked.

"Only to take his order. He wasn't in a talkative mood. He did make some snarky comment about my food tasting a small step above the savage's, whatever that was supposed to mean."

I looked at Vance. "He was probably referring to the meat-on-a-stick thing."

Vance turned to his mom and filled her in on Terry's booth.

"Got it. That would make sense, then." Heather looked over her shoulder and held up the coffee pot. "Be right there," she said to another table.

"Real quick. Did he have a coffee cup with him?" I asked.

"A coffee cup? Like a mug?" Heather asked.

"No, like a to-go cup from Diane's," I explained.

"No, not at all. Why do you ask?"

I kept my voice low. "Because he was found with a pumpkin spice latte in his hand, and it turns out it was poisoned."

Heather shook her head. "No, as a matter of fact, he ordered a cup of coffee here and a slice of pie."

I turned to Vance, unsure of what that might mean. Diane had finished selling coffee by nine o'clock. Her staff packed up their booth right after that, and she was sitting around the bonfire with us.

"One minute. I'll be right back." Heather went and refilled the other table's mugs, and I shared my thoughts with Vance.

"When did he get the coffee cup from Diane, then?" Vance asked.

"That's what I'm wondering."

"Okay, I'm back." Heather returned. "Before I

forget, I wanted to tell you what was strange about it. You know Dolores Zilinsky?"

Vance and I nodded. Dolores was a retiree who still worked part-time at the supermarket. She always said hello and chatted while ringing up my groceries. She would ask about Aunt Thelma or Vance and genuinely seemed interested in the response. "I like Dolores. She's always so friendly."

"Right, which makes her behavior toward Mr. Haggerty so odd. It might not be anything, but the two shared a look. I got the feeling there was more there, especially after she requested the rest of her dessert to go and left promptly after. Might be worth looking into."

Vance and I shared a look. We'd be heading there shortly. "She lives in the duplex across from Loretta Johnson. The one with the scarecrow in the yard."

I shuddered at the scarecrow reference. I never liked them to begin with, but now they gave me the chills ever since I saw one come to life one Halloween. That sort of image tended to stay with you forever.

Thankfully, Heather knew Diane and Roger's go-to breakfast order and was more than happy to put it together. "On the house," Heather said as she handed the bag over. "Tell Diane to give me a call if she'd like lunch, too."

"Will do," I said as we left the diner and made our way around the lake to the community hospital.

I used to say one of the nicest things about living in Silverlake was that you come to know a lot of people in the community, and everyone really cared for one another. Well, that's the way it used to be. With the theft of the sapphire and Mr. Haggerty's death, I really wasn't sure anymore.

It turned out that Luke's sister, Sally, was Roger's nurse. The twins' mother was coming out of his room as Vance and I were approaching it. Deputy Lopez was sitting outside the door.

She smiled at us, and I replied with a head nod.

"I'm so glad I ran into you." Sally used the hand sanitizer on the outside of the door. "The girls told me about what happened last night with the jewelry. I'm so sorry!"

"Oh, it's not your fault. I should have described the sapphire better or something." If I had been thinking, we would have practiced the summoning charm on something close by, something that we could all see, so the girls could see the way the spell worked. I clearly hadn't been thinking straight. "On the bright side, they haven't lost their iPad since." Sally smiled. "I should have taught a summoning charm to them years ago. Would've saved me time finding their electronics all these years."

"How's Roger doing?" Vance asked.

"He's resting now, but Diane's in there."

"Can we talk to her?" I asked the question to both Sally and Deputy Lopez.

"They're good. I can vouch for them," Sally directed her comment to the deputy.

"Go on in," Deputy Lopez replied.

"Thanks." I waved bye to Sally.

Vance slowly opened the heavy wooden door, and we slipped inside.

The hospital room's lights were off. The only light coming in was from the room's window, which Diane was staring out. Her back was to us, and her arms were folded across her chest. She appeared lost in thought. Roger was asleep, and I was careful to keep my voice low. "Hey, is this a bad time?"

Diane turned at the sound of my voice. "No, come in," her voice was merely a whisper. "He just fell asleep."

"Brought you guys some breakfast, compliments of Heather." I placed the bag on the counter.

"Do you want to step out in the hallway?" Vance offered. I knew what he was thinking. He didn't want to wake Roger.

"I'd rather not if that's okay." Diane looked back at Roger.

"How are you doing?" I asked.

"I'm okay. Still in shock a bit. Can't imagine why someone would want to burn down the flower shop."

"We can. It turns out that poison used to kill Mr. Haggerty comes from a black orchid that Roger had," Vance explained.

"We think that whoever the killer is, they either bought the flower from him or they stole it, and your cameras caught the transaction," I continued.

"Which is why the fire started in the back room with your security equipment," Vance added.

"The evidence has been destroyed?" Diane asked.

"Afraid so. We are hoping that when Roger wakes up, he might remember if he sold an orchid to anyone." I looked over at Roger, who was resting comfortably.

"I would wake him, but he barely got any sleep last night. Sally gave him some medicine a little bit ago to help settle him."

"No, let him rest. But will you ask him when he wakes up?" Vance asked.

"Absolutely. I'll call you right away."

"Did he, by chance, say anything about the fire?" I asked.

"No. The only thing he remembers is locking up. The person attacked him from behind." Diane looked distraught. No one needed to point out the person started the fire and left Roger for dead.

"We'll find out whoever did this. I promise." I reached over and gave Diane's hand a squeeze. "You make sure to take care of yourself, too. Eat something," I motioned to the food on the counter.

"And my mom said to call her for lunch," Vance added.

"Thank you, both of you. I'll call you once Roger is awake."

Chapter 13

Vance's plan to accompany me to Dolores's changed. Deputy Jones called on our way out of the hospital to say the sheriff planned to formally question Diane again.

"What in the world for? Her husband was almost killed last night. Now is not the time," Vance had replied.

The deputy agreed with him, hence the phone call. Vance turned around and went back into the hospital. He wasn't about to let the sheriff ambush Diane now.

That was how I found myself fifteen minutes later parking on the road in front of Dolores's house solo. I gave the scarecrow the side eye and a wide berth as I kept to the far end of the walkway and jogged up the steps to the front porch. I knocked on the metal storm door and was instantly greeted by a round of yaps from the front window. I took a step back and peeked inside. A yorkie stood on the back of the couch, barking at me for all he was worth.

"You be quiet, Sargent. We have ourselves a visitor," Dolores's voice came from inside. "Angelica Nightingale. Well, this is a surprise."

"I wondered if you had a few minutes to chat?"

"Oh, you know me. I always have a few minutes to chat. Come on in." The older woman opened her front door the rest of the way. Sargent, the Yorkie, growled at me and gave a couple of added yaps for good measure. "You cut that out right now," Dolores told her fearless companion as she led me through the front living room and into her kitchen.

"I was just going to put on some tea. Would you like some?"

"Sure, that would be great." I wasn't much of a tea drinker, but I found that it helped always to accept whatever hospitality someone extended you. It went a long way in opening up the lines of communication.

"What can I do for you? Did you want to volunteer for the bazaar?" Dolores asked.

"The Christmas bazaar?"

"You know, the one that's at the high school every year? I'm chairing it this year."

"No, I know all about the bazaar. But that's not why I'm here. I was wondering if you knew anything about the journalist who passed away in town Friday night, Mr. David Haggerty? I'm trying to piece together his last twenty-four hours, and I was told you saw him late that evening."

Dolores took a steadying breath. "I suppose I shouldn't be surprised that you heard about that. David always had a way of getting under my skin."

"You knew him?"

"I did. Let me get that tea."

I waited patiently while Dolores poured the boiling water from the kettle into the teapot and brought the entire set to the kitchen table. "Now then, where were we?"

"You knew David Haggerty," I started for her.

"Right." Dolores closed her eyes. When she opened them, she said, "David Haggerty was my nephew."

"Your nephew? I didn't realize he had any family in town. I'm so sorry for your loss."

"It's quite all right. We weren't close. Not anymore."

"You two had a falling out." It was a statement and not a question.

Dolores poured two cups of tea. "Sugar?" she asked.

"Yes, please."

"Sorry, I should've asked if you wanted any milk. I have some in the fridge."

"No, the sugar is great."

Again, I waited for Dolores to continue the story. It took her a moment to gather her resolve.

"I hadn't spoken with David in over eight years. When his mother died, he sued his father, my brother, for more money."

"That's awful."

"Indeed, it was. David felt his father misinterpreted the will. The instructions stated he was entitled to what his father thought he deserved."

"It was open to interpretation?"

Dolores nodded. "His mother always hoped David would redeem himself."

"How so?"

"Once David's journalism career took off, he couldn't be bothered with his family. The visits grew further and further apart. Eventually, he quit coming home altogether and then stopped calling for holidays and birthdays. It was like he cut his family out of his life."

I could relate. I'd practically done the same thing, hadn't I? I didn't like the thought of Mr. Haggerty and I having something in common. I took a sip of tea to hide my thoughts.

"He didn't even come home when his mother died. I was amazed my brother thought David deserved anything."

"I see." At least I'd come running when I thought Aunt Thelma was dying. I gave myself a mental shake. This wasn't about me. I needed to focus on the case. "And where is your brother now?"

"He's passed on, I'm afraid. The two never made amends. Last I heard, David was fighting my brother's will as well. You see, my brother didn't leave him a dime, and I don't blame him." Dolores became teary-eyed. "Sorry, I didn't think I was that upset, but I suppose I am."

"David was still part of your family, and deep wounds take a long time to heal."

"Thank you for saying that. I guess I do need to give myself some grace."

I gave Dolores a moment to collect herself.

"Does this all mean that David was an only child?"

Dolores took a sip of her tea before answering me. "He was. He did marry, but that was years ago. It was short-lived. He never had any kids, either. I'd read an article of his every now and then, but truthfully, I was too disappointed in him to follow his career much."

"I bet you were surprised to see him in town."

"Not as much as he was surprised to see me. By the look on his face, he didn't even know I lived here."

"Did you get a chance to talk with him?"

A tear rolled down Dolores's cheek.

"I'm sorry. You don't have to answer. I didn't mean to be insensitive."

"It's alright. He came through my line at the store last week. I think we were both shocked to see one another. He pretended like he didn't know who I was, even though I saw the spark of recognition in his eyes. He treated me like I was no one, complained about the store's inventory, and then left without a backward glance."

"I'm so sorry he treated you that way."

"You can see why I wasn't so happy to see him Friday night at the diner. That's where you heard I ran into him, wasn't it?"

I nodded.

"The whole situation breaks my heart. I always hoped David would realize what he lost after his mother passed away and then after his father died. But no, he was coldhearted right to the end."

"Again, I am sorry for your loss. If you need anything, let me know."

"That's a very sweet thing for you to offer. But I'll be all right. I've made peace with a lot of things in my life; this is just another one to add to the list."

"I've never thought of heartbreak that way before."

"Let me tell you; you don't get to be my age without being a survivor." Dolores nodded and then moved to refill her teacup.

"Thank you for chatting with me. I guess I better be going."

"Thank you for looking into David's death. I hope you find out who did this."

"I'm sure going to try. Have a nice day, Dolores, and thank you for the tea."

Dolores moved to stand up. "No, sit. Enjoy your tea. I'll see myself out."

"Goodbye then, and stop by anytime. I almost always have the kettle on."

"I'll keep that in mind. See you soon."

Chapter 14

Aunt Thelma called me as I was walking back to the car. "There's someone on their way to the inn that I think you should talk to," she said after our lines connected.

"Who is it?"

"Mr. Haggerty's editor. His name's Thomas Crum. He came to track down his journalist after Mr. Haggerty quit returning calls. I just broke the news of his passing. I didn't tell him any other details. He's getting his bags now."

"I'll be there in ten minutes."

Amelia was entertaining our new guest when I walked into the lobby.

"A Pulitzer Prize? Are you certain?" The man, who I presumed to be the editor for *Witch Reader's Magazine*, bent forward to get on the same level as the young psychic.

"Yes, but it's not going to be where you're at now. You're going to have to go work for the mortals in order to land the prize."

"Interesting. I'll keep it in mind."

"Good luck! It was nice meeting you." Amelia waved enthusiastically to the editor and then turned to meet the twins. Beatrice and Sabrina were waiting nearby. The trio walked out of the lobby together, talking a mile a minute.

"It seems like Amelia is happier," I said to my aunt.

"I talked to her mom earlier, and she said that Amelia likes telling fortunes, but only when they're good."

"Downfall to the profession, I suppose. If only there were a way she could choose what she saw."

"What did you say?" Aunt Thelma asked. It was a rhetorical question. I could tell by the twinkle in her eye.

"What are you thinking?"

"I'm not sure yet, but I'll let you know when I figure things out." The editor approached the registration desk. "Mr. Crum, this here's my niece, Angelica, who I was telling you about. She's been working with the sheriff's department and finding out what happened to your journalist." I smiled at my aunt. If only the sheriff's department considered my interfering in their cases as helping.

"I'm very sorry for your loss," I said after shaking Thomas's hand.

"Thank you so much. I hate to say it, but I'm not surprised. I always knew David's mouth would get him in trouble. If he hadn't been such a good writer, I would've fired him years ago. Can't help but feel a bit responsible."

"Because you didn't fire him?" I asked.

"For sending him here. I knew it was a mistake. A man like David Haggerty didn't appreciate the simple things in life. But I was short-staffed, and I thought if I sent Catherine along, the two could work together. Is she around?"

"Who?" I asked.

"Catherine Kelly. She's the other journalist judging the town," Thomas clarified.

"Catherine? I don't know a Catherine." I turned to my aunt to see if she knew who Thomas was referring to. "Mr. Haggerty checked in solo," I explained.

Aunt Thelma tapped her chin. "But you know what, there was a reservation for a Catherine Kelly now that you mention it. She never checked in."

"What do you mean she never checked in?" Thomas asked.

"She was a no-show." Aunt Thelma looked down at the calendar as if she was looking for a note but came up empty. "No phone call or anything; she forfeited her deposit, and I charged her for the first night."

"That doesn't make sense. If you will excuse me, I'm going to see if I can reach my junior editor." Thomas stepped away and walked toward the lobby's seating area. Aunt Thelma had started the fire while I was out and added a couple of fleece throws to the back of the brown leather couch, creating a comfy scene. I'd love to wrap up on the sofa with a cup of hot cider and a good book if I wasn't solving a murder.

We tried not to eavesdrop, but Thomas's voice carried courtesy of the lobby's vaulted ceiling. From the sounds of it, his junior editor hadn't heard from Catherine.

"That doesn't sound good. I wonder if this mystery woman is the one who killed Mr. Haggerty?"

"I don't know, maybe." I had to admit that I liked the idea of someone from outside Silverlake being responsible for Mr. Haggerty's death.

"Speaking of Mr. Haggerty, I was thinking about how no one saw him with the coffee cup Friday night. What if he went out Saturday morning? He could've walked out of his room's sliding glass door and got a cup of coffee without any of us seeing him."

"And leave his door unlocked? That doesn't sound like him," Aunt Thelma remarked. She was right. I said as much. If Mr. Haggerty had gone out his sliding glass door, he wouldn't have been able to lock it behind him.

We were both quiet for a moment while we thought things through.

"I think we're making this harder than it has to be," I said. "Maybe Mr. Haggerty walked right through the lobby and out the front door. Where's Percy?" Lately, I saw his wife more than our resident poltergeist, but he had to be around somewhere. Percy worked the midnight shift. He always had for as long as I could remember.

"He popped off to visit his brother in Idaho. There was a birthday party amongst the living that he thought he could crash. Something about a great, great nephew."

"He worked Friday night through Saturday morning, though, didn't he?"

"He did, but only until about seven o'clock. Emily came in after that."

Emily worked part-time at the inn and had since picked up more hours. She might be young, but she had a solid work ethic. She was an early riser too, which suited me just fine. I preferred working midmorning through late afternoon. "Let me call her and see if she remembers seeing Mr. Haggerty come through."

I took out my cell phone and did just that. I wasn't surprised when Emily answered right away.

Her punctuality was one of the reasons why I hired her. That and perhaps she reminded me a bit of myself.

"Hey, Angelica. Is everything okay?" my employee asked.

"Yes and no."

"Oh? Do you need me to come in? I can't right now, but I'm free in an hour."

"No, it's not that. You heard about our guest that passed away, right?" Emily had left before we discovered the body, but I had assumed she would have heard about it through the grapevine.

"What? No! I left town yesterday and spent the night up at Georgia State. I'm almost back now. We had a guest pass away?"

"It was Mr. Haggerty. You know that journalist."

"I know who you're talking about. Wow, I can't believe that. How did he die?"

"I can fill you in on that later, but right now, we're trying to find out if you saw him yesterday morning when you were working. The sheriff is trying to determine the time of death." Okay, I was trying to determine the time of death, but I was sure the sheriff wanted to know too.

"Let me think about it." I gave Emily a thinking minute. "You know what, I did. He came through the lobby, probably around eight o'clock. I'm not positive, but it was before your aunt came down for the morning, and she's usually behind the desk by eight thirty."

"You did? Do you know if he had a cup of coffee with them?"

"Eh … I think so? I'm not positive because it always seemed like he had a coffee cup with him."

"It did?"

"At least every morning I saw him," Emily commented.

"Okay, you've been very helpful. Thank you so much. Drive safe, and I'll see you, what, tomorrow morning?"

"Bright and early," Emily said, and then we hung up.

Aunt Thelma looked at me expectantly.

"What did she say?"

"She saw him before you came down for the morning, and she thinks he had a cup of coffee with him."

"Looks like you narrowed down the time of death."

"I know." I stood lost in my thoughts.

"But?" She could tell I had a lot on my mind.

"I'm torn. Do I hunt down this Catherine person, retrace Mr. Haggerty's final hours, or should I look for the sapphire?" I hadn't forgotten about the missing gemstone.

"Leave the sapphire to the town council. I'm not

as worried about it as I was last night," Aunt Thelma confessed.

"How come?" I wondered what could possibly have changed in the past twelve hours.

"I forgot about the precautions we added after the last theft attempt until Mike McCormick caught up and reminded me."

"Added precautions? Like what?" They couldn't have been too effective if someone had still been able to steal it.

"It's top-secret, official council business. I could tell you about it if you were a member..." Aunt Thelma allowed her sentence to trail off. It was no secret she wanted me to run for a spot on the council, but I thought one Nightingale on the committee was plenty. "I wouldn't have said anything except I know how you worry."

"So, you don't want me looking for the sapphire?"

"Don't stick your head in the sand or anything. If you hear something, I expect you to look into it, but no need to go hunting for clues. I have a feeling the sapphire will turn up when it's supposed to."

"Well, that isn't cryptic or anything," I replied dryly.

"Now, where is my wand?" Aunt Thelma patted her pockets and smoothed out her hair. She was known to use it like a hairpin from time to time, but she came up empty.

"You misplaced it again?"

"Don't look at me like that. Studies show that people who frequently misplace things are creative geniuses."

"You just made that up."

"Hm, prove it." Aunt Thelma lifted the desk calendar to look under it, followed by the computer keyboard.

"I thought you put a charm on it so you'd be able to find it?"

"I took it off." Aunt Thelma tapped her temple. "Finding things helps keep your mind sharp."

I shook my head. "You don't have another bowl of pretzels lying around, do you?"

"Aren't you cute."

"I'm being serious."

Aunt Thelma slipped into the back office and returned with her purse. She unceremoniously dumped it on the counter. Out fell a half-eaten candy bar, two tubes of lipstick, a pack of bubblegum, her wallet, and a gold watch. "Oh look, my watch and my favorite lipstick! I was wondering where they went to. Everything I need except for my wand." Aunt Thelma drummed her fingers on the countertop.

"Where did you have it last?" It always helped me to retrace my steps.

Aunt Thelma snapped her fingers. "Oh, I know. She turned around to the office, and this time, I followed her. Aunt Thelma pulled open the desk drawer and retrieved a romance novel. Her wand was tucked safely in between the pages. "I needed a bookmark."

"Of course you did."

"What? It worked."

"You could've used a piece of paper, an envelope, a receipt. Look around. It's an office. There's paper everywhere," But Aunt Thelma wasn't listening to me. She was too busy reading her book.

Chapter 15

I looked down at my phone and saw that Luke had just sent me a text message asking me to call him when I got a minute. There was no time like the present, so I quickly returned his call.

"Sorry, I didn't know if you were free, but I got a tip. We were cleaning up at the fire station last night when … hang on." I could still hear Luke in the background. "Girls, drop your wands. You don't need magic. Just use a spatula. Girls. Girls? Hey, you're not listening. No magic back here. Don't use your wands. Girls, listen. Wait!" Luke's pleas were answered by the sound of breaking glass, followed by a loud clatter, a couple of shrieks, and a round of apologies. "We're so sorry, Uncle Luke! Please don't be mad! We'll clean it up. It was an accident!"

Guess I knew where the twins and Amelia had run off to.

"My chili is ruined," Luke said to himself more than anyone.

I looked at the clock. The chili cookoff was starting in a few hours. I'd completely forgotten about the town picnic and competition.

"Luke, are you there?"

"Huh? Oh, sorry. Yeah, I'm here."

"How about I come to you? I can help you clean up, and you can fill me in on what you heard." I could tell Luke wanted to argue, but he did have his hands full, and this would be easier.

"Okay. You'll probably want to be in Village Square anyway once I fill you in."

That sounded intriguing. "I'm on my way." I turned to my aunt. "I'm headed to the Candy Cauldron. If Thomas says anything about Catherine, let me know. I'll be back shortly."

If I had time, I'd take Enchanted Trail, but I didn't. So I drove the short distance around the lake and searched the parking lot for an empty spot. I was tempted to park in the grass after searching in vain for an open space, but I knew I'd end up with a ticket. The town council had set up tents across the street at Wishing Well Park. They were red-and-white striped and reminded me of the circus. The council had also set up rows of folding tables and chairs underneath the tents, giving people a place to sit if they didn't want to unfold a blanket in the grass. Eating chili on the ground could be a bit tricky.

My eyes were drawn back to the parking lot. It took me a second to realize why. "Ah-ha!" I spotted brake lights one row in front of me, a telltale sign someone was backing up. But when I drove around, Terry Dawes's big red diesel truck beat me to it. "Darn it!" I tried not to frown. It wasn't his fault that he got to it first.

I was still idling in the traffic lane, looking for another spot, when Terry approached my car. I didn't see him at first. I was too busy looking out my windshield when he knocked on my driver's side window.

"Ah!" I jumped away from the window and looked over my shoulder at the same time. My heart rate didn't slow down even after I realized who it was. Terry glowered at me. His muscular arms were folded across his broad chest.

I cautiously rolled down the window.

"Hi, Terry. What can I do for you?"

"For starters, you can tell that candy maker friend of yours to stop following me."

"Do you mean Luke?"

"Whatever his name is. He's following me, and I don't like it."

"Oh, um, okay." I wasn't sure what else to say. As far as I knew, Luke had only followed Terry the one time.

"I didn't kill that journalist, and I don't need any trouble. Do you understand?" Terry's words held a threatening undertone.

"Absolutely."

"If you ask me, that man got what he deserved. I take that back. He should've got kicked in the teeth a time or two."

I nodded because, really, how was I supposed to respond to that?

I looked forward and saw someone else backing up. "Oh! If you'll excuse me. I see a spot. I want to nab it before it gets taken." I didn't give Terry much time to respond before I inched off the break and coasted away.

I couldn't help looking over my shoulder as I hightailed it through Village Square. There was no denying it; Terry Dawes scared me.

The girls met me out front of the Candy Cauldron when I arrived. I had originally wanted to stop by and see what Roger's shop looked like, but the fire department still had it sectioned off, and I didn't want to get in trouble going under the barrier. It would just be my luck that Amber would be standing guard or something like that, and I'd only end up making things worse. Besides, there wasn't much I'd be able to garner from looking at the shop. It wasn't like I was a fire investigator. It was more like morbid curiosity.

"Blue!" Beatrice pointed her wand at her sister and changed her hair to a vibrant ocean blue.

"Pink!" Sabrina returned the favor, but only to Amelia.

"Green!" Amelia pointed her wand at Beatrice and changed her hair to the color of lime Jell-O.

"Hey! It's Angelica. Did you find the sapphire?" Beatrice asked. All three girls stared at me in anticipation.

"Not yet, but I know the town council is working very hard on it."

The girls did not look impressed. "I thought you said she was going to find it." Amelia said to the twins as if I wasn't standing right there.

"I thought she would. It's not like Angelica to ignore a case," Sabrina replied.

"Maybe she only likes to solve murders," Beatrice suggested.

"Girls, I'm standing right here," I pointed out.

"It's because that journalist died, isn't it?" Beatrice put her hand on her hip.

"David the Downer. I bet loads of people wanted to kill him," Sabrina added.

"We heard our mom talking to Uncle Luke all about it. You're too busy working that case, aren't you?" Beatrice accused.

"That's part of it," I answered honestly.

"That settles it, then. We need to figure out who

killed the journalist, and then Angelica can find the sapphire!" Sabrina exclaimed.

"Wait! I forbid you from looking into Mr. Haggerty's death. It is extremely dangerous, and there is no way that either of your mothers would want you anywhere near that case." I pointed my finger at each one of the girls in succession. In hindsight, that was probably the worst thing to do, as they seemed even more eager to crack the case. I had to go about this differently.

I quickly changed tactics, "Besides, I have another top-secret case that I need your help with." That stopped the girls in their tracks. Unfortunately, it required me to think fast because I could not think of a single thing I needed their help with.

"See, the thing is…it's not really the journalist's death keeping me from searching for the sapphire." I was winging it here.

"It's not?" The girls looked skeptical.

"No, not at all. You see, I'm getting married."

"When?" Beatrice asked me.

"Soon-ish," I added the -ish part a beat later.

"Uh-huh." Sabrina did not believe me.

"She is. I saw it, except…" Amelia let her words trail off.

"Except what?" I asked.

"It's nothing." But based on the look on Amelia's face, it wasn't nothing. It was something important, and I wanted to know what it was.

"You can tell me. I promise I won't be mad at you," I tried to reason. Amelia bit her bottom lip. She looked like she might cry. I tried to backtrack. "Hey, if you don't want to, that's okay. I don't want you to be upset."

"I want to tell you, but I don't want to make you worry," Amelia's voice wobbled.

I had lied.

Now I *had* to know what the poor girl saw. I would go nuts until I found out.

I tried to keep my expression as encouraging as possible. "Maybe if you tell me what you see, I might be able to fix it. I'll listen to you, I promise."

"No one ever listens to me," Amelia had such a sorrowful expression. It tugged right at my heart-strings.

"I will this time. That's a promise." I held my pinky out for Amelia to hook hers with mine so I could swear on it.

"Go on. You can trust Angelica," Beatrice said.

"Yeah, she's one of the good ones," Sabrina added.

"Thanks, girls," I said to the twins.

Amelia seemed to make up her mind and latched her pinkie onto mine, and we shook on it.

"Tell me, what did you see?"

"Okay, the thing is, there is someone who doesn't want you to get married. I can't see who it is, but they don't like you, and it's going to make you sad," Amelia winced. Even Beatrice and Sabrina looked like they felt sorry for me.

"And this person is going to try to stop the wedding?" I took a guess.

"Uh-huh," Amelia nodded. "I'm sorry. I hope you still want to get married."

"You better get married. I like Vance!" Beatrice said.

"I do too. He's handsome," Sabrina said.

"And he's never scared to try our chocolates." Beatrice gave me a level stare. You couldn't get anything past those girls.

"Don't worry. We're not going to call off the wedding. It just means we will have to keep the wedding plans a secret. Do you think you guys can help me do that?" The girls all nodded. "Perfect, because that's what I need your help with. I want you guys to make chocolates for the wedding. Whatever flavors you want. We can pass them out as favors.

"Favors?" Sabrina scrunched her nose.

"It means they'll be a little gift for the wedding guests, and I'll make sure everyone knows you made them. How does that sound?"

"Hang on a minute. We need to talk it over," Beatrice replied.

I tried not to chuckle as the trio turned their backs to me and got into a huddle. Their voices whispered back and forth as they debated my offer.

"How many chocolates did you say you needed?" Beatrice asked.

"Hmm, let me think." I really had no clue, but guests would probably want more than one. "How about two hundred?"

Beatrice turned back around.

Again, there was more whispering; this time, it was Sabrina who asked a question. "Can we make them any flavor we want?"

"Sure, as long as they taste good."

"Well, duh," Sabrina rolled her eyes.

I took a deep breath and reminded myself that I was just trying to keep the young witches out of trouble. Making chocolates was far safer than tracking down a killer.

Finally, they were done deliberating.

"Okay, we'll do it!" Beatrice said.

"We're going to get started experimenting with new flavors right away," Sabrina said.

They looked back at the Candy Cauldron. Hesitation filled their expressions as they probably remembered the mess they'd recently made. "Maybe we should do it back home?" Beatrice suggested.

"Good idea. Come on, Amelia, let's go." Sabrina hooked her arm through her new friend's.

Oh, to be young again, I thought as they skipped off. Those girls had boundless energy and enthusiasm.

Inside, I waved to Luke's staff as I slipped my way back to his kitchen.

"I'm impressed. It doesn't look too bad at all." Luke was on a ladder wiping the remaining mess off the ceiling tiles.

"You should have seen it a half hour ago. Those girls are lucky I had two pots of chili, and they only ruined one." Luke stepped off the ladder.

"So, what did you want to tell me about?"

"Wait, where did the girls go?"

"They're headed home to make chocolates. I hope that's okay?"

Luke looked up at the clock. "Yeah, their mom got out of work about thirty minutes ago. She should be home by now, but just in case, let me text her so she doesn't run any errands." Luke did just that and then said, "Okay, so like I was saying, last night we were at the fire station talking about everything, and my buddy Paul saw Mr. Haggerty leave Cassidy's shop early Saturday morning."

"The healer."

"Mmm-hmm."

"What was Mr. Haggerty doing visiting her?"

"I don't know, but Paul said it was early, like sunrise early."

I thought about what time the sun was currently rising and figured it had to be just before seven. "Interesting. Okay, I guess I'm going to visit Cassidy."

"Yeah, I thought you might want to."

"If anything, she can help piece together Mr. Haggerty's final hours and let me know if he had that coffee cup with him or not."

"I'd offer to come with you, but…" Luke looked longingly at his pot of chili simmering on the stove.

"No, it's okay. I'll just pop in and talk to Cassidy."

"If you're sure?"

"I am. Good luck with the cook-off today. I'll try to stop out."

"That would be great. Hopefully, I'll see you in a bit."

Chapter 16

I thought of something as I was weaving down the cobblestone path of Village Square. I didn't want to bother Diane, but this was too important to wait. I quickly texted my friend and asked her if she had a moment to talk. I didn't want to call and wake Roger.

Diane replied by calling me. "Hi, what's going on?" She spoke at her normal volume, meaning she was either outside Roger's room or he was awake.

"How's Roger doing?"

"He's doing better. They just took him for a CAT scan to check for swelling. I think he'll be back soon."

"Let me know when you guys hear something."

"Of course. I'll send a group text."

"That would be great."

"So, what's going on?"

"You're not going to believe this. We found out Mr. Haggerty was alive yesterday morning. One of Luke's friends saw him leave Cassidy's shop around sunrise, and Emily remembers seeing him come back to the inn."

"Sunrise, huh?"

"I know. I'm stopping by Cassidy's to ask her about it. But in the meantime, is there a way you can check your camera footage from Saturday morning? I hate to ask, but I think it's important."

Diane sighed. "I should've figured it was connected."

"What are you talking about?"

"There's no footage from Saturday."

An ambulance siren wailed in the distance, and it was hard for me to hear Diane. "Come again?"

"The footage stops Saturday morning before seven o'clock."

"The killer turned the cameras off?" I wanted to make sure I understood what Diane was saying.

"Or they erased the footage."

"Who was working yesterday?"

"Anna and Kellan. The sheriff already interviewed them, and they didn't know what had happened. Anna said everything seemed normal when she opened up for the day and never thought to check the cameras, which is normal. The system's in my office, and they never go back there."

"The killer must've snuck in and tampered with your equipment when nobody was looking."

"They must've. I didn't think much of it when we thought Mr. Haggerty had died Friday night. It was unfortunate the cameras had quit working, but it wasn't important."

"Whoever the killer is, they're smart. I feel like we're always one step behind."

"Do you think it means Mr. Haggerty was poisoned at the bakery?" Diane asked.

"I think it's a solid possibility."

"But how?"

"You sure it's not Anna or Kellan?"

"I'd be shocked. I can't see that at all. No, I bet the killer slipped something in his drink, maybe at the bakery, but it wasn't those two."

"I don't know."

"What was that?" It was Diane's turn to ask me to repeat myself. There were more sirens passing by. "Sorry, there must be an accident. It's really loud. I'm going to go and talk to Cassidy. I'll call you back." I practically shouted into the phone.

"Okay, sounds good. And I'll let you know what they say about Roger."

"Good deal."

By the time I hung up with Diane, I was standing in front of Cassidy's shop, only the welcome sign was switched to closed, and the lights were turned off. I knocked on the glass window pane on the door and used my hand to shield my eyes so I could peer in. "Cassidy? Are you in there?"

I saw a light coming from the back hallway and hoped that meant she was in the back working in her office. Stepping back, I read the shop's hours on the door's sign. She should be open right now. I twisted the doorknob, but it was locked tight. I sighed in frustration. It would've been nice if Cassidy had been here. Seeing she was new in town, I didn't know where she lived, and I wasn't sure who to ask. Her shop didn't list a phone number, and I wasn't sure if she was close to anyone in town. I tried to think of who I'd seen her talk with, and Roger was the only person who came to mind.

I was ready to turn to walk away when I noticed movement in the front window followed by a meow. The gray cat bumped his head on the glass and meowed some more as if saying hello.

Suddenly, from inside the shop, I heard someone say, "Sir Whiskers!" followed by a whistle. The kitty turned toward his name but stopped short of hopping down. Instead, the kitty turned back and eyed an aloe plant that was also in the window.

"No, no, kitty!" I said to the gray furball as he bent low and began nibbling on the corner of the stalk. I didn't know if aloe was toxic to cats, but it couldn't taste good. Judging by the face Sir Whiskers made, I was right. The cat stuck out his tongue and opened his mouth repeatedly as if he wanted to get the taste out of his mouth. I knocked louder on the window, "Cassidy! Your cat!" hoping she would hear me, but all I managed to do was startle Sir Whiskers. Instead of running away, he bumped into the plant's clay pot and sent it crashing to the ground. That made him skitter off and caused Cassidy to run out.

I waved from the window to get her attention. Cassidy tried to ignore me, but it was too late. We clearly saw one another.

Sir Whiskers appeared at the door and rubbed himself along the frame, continuing to meow.

Begrudgingly, she came to the door. Her eyes were puffy as if she had been crying. "I'm sorry, I'm closed today," she said through the door.

"I need to talk to you. This will only take a minute, I promise. It's really important."

Cassidy unlocked the deadbolt and partially opened the door. I noticed Cassidy wasn't inviting me in, but her gray kitty looked like he would love to have me come in and give him some pets. He continued to meow and weave in and out of Cassidy's legs.

"First, your cat—did you say his name was Sir Whiskers?"

Cassidy nodded.

"Okay, he was eating an aloe plant in the window. Only a little bit, but I wanted you to know."

Cassidy looked down at her feline. "Sir Whiskers, we talked about this. It'll give you a tummy ache." Cassidy looked at me. "He's a troublesome fluff ball, but I love him," she sniffled.

Sir Whiskers looked up. "Meow?"

"That was the crash you heard. He knocked the plant out of the window."

Sir Whiskers then turned his attention to me and gave me the stink eye as if he couldn't believe I had ratted him out. I started to second-guess if the cat was really a cat after all. Perhaps he was a witch in disguise or a shifter? You never knew around here. I bent down to scratch his ears. He replied with a love bite. He was a troublesome fella, alright.

"Thanks for letting me know." Cassidy turned to shut the door.

"Wait." I stood so that I was back to eye level with her. "I also wanted to talk to you real quick about Mr. Haggerty."

That turned out to be the wrong thing to say. The moment the man's name left my lips, Cassidy burst into tears.

"Hey, it's okay." My mind raced, wondering if Cassidy had been close to the man or why else she might be crying.

"No, it's not. You don't understand. I killed him."

"What?" I took a step back.

"I didn't mean to. It was an honest mistake." I

looked around to see how many people were listening in on our conversation and decided it would be better if we took it someplace private. Given Cassidy's reaction, I didn't think she was the killer for one second. No, the killer was someone who was relentless. They destroyed evidence and lives. They weren't apologetic.

"Can I come in?"

Cassidy nodded and backed up, letting me into her shop. The place was soothing, with wide planked oak floors and whitewashed walls. Glass bottles in different shapes and sizes lined the shelves, full of dried herbs and flowers. A mixture of plants and climbing vines shared the space and added a soothing effect. The air smelled earthy, like after a fresh rain when the soil was still damp. Sir Whiskers looked up at me and meowed as if asking what was wrong with his owner.

"It's okay, buddy. We'll figure this out," I replied to him.

I followed Cassidy over to her workstation. She began halfheartedly grinding rose petals with a mortar and pestle, barely putting any energy into working the grinder.

"Do you think a jury will go easy on me?"

"Why do you think you killed Mr. Haggerty?"

"It's my restorative tonic. I didn't make it right. I just found out that he was poisoned. It has to be from me. Sometimes I mess up. Sir Whiskers distracts me." The cat meowed at the mention of his name.

"Yes, he was poisoned, but I don't think it was from you. What's in the tonic?"

"Let's see, tart cherry, Siberian ginseng, lemon balm, passionflower."

I nodded as Cassidy ticked the entire ingredient list off. I noted the midnight orchid was not one of them.

"And did you give him this tonic just Saturday morning?"

"Oh no, he stopped in and saw me the first night he was in town. He was sick." Cassidy thought about it for a minute. "I suppose I can tell you about it seeing he's now passed.'

I nodded encouragingly.

"He had a progressive condition that was getting worse. He was desperate to stop it, but unfortunately, I didn't have the cure. He was mad at first, but then he came back, willing to try anything I had that might slow it."

"Was it terminal?

Cassidy nodded. "Slowly, and it was eating away at him. He didn't want to accept it."

"I'm not sure I'd want to either."

"No, I'd fight with everything I had too, but hopefully, I'd be a bit nicer along the way.

I was starting to think that Mr. Haggerty's foul mood reflected more of his trials than anything else.

"I supplied him with the tonic all week, except he ran out Friday night, and I was closed for the parade. He told me he was leaving town the next morning and asked if he could stop by early and pick it up."

"Was it a different batch or the same one all week?"

"The same batch. I haven't sold a lot of it. I was hoping once Mr. Haggerty's article was published, word-of-mouth would get around, and business would pick up."

I hated to tell Cassidy that Mr. Haggerty's article was not flattering in the least bit, but I decided against it. He was probably angry that she couldn't provide a cure. "Listen, you didn't kill him. The poison? It was from a midnight orchid."

"Midnight orchid? Those are super toxic. I don't go anywhere near them."

I raised my eyebrows as if to say *see?*

"Those are the orchids Roger had at his flower shop, right?"

"Mmm-hm."

"And someone tried to burn down the flower shop."

"Yeah." I didn't elaborate. Cassidy was doing a fine job putting things together on her own. "You think the killer used one of Roger's orchids and then burned down the shop to destroy the evidence?"

"You got it. Now you see why you didn't kill him?"

"I didn't kill him? I really didn't?"

"No, but you might want to lock Sir Whiskers up next time you're working." The kitty had jumped up onto Cassie's workstation and was about to knock over a stopper full of gold liquid. Heaven only knew what was in it. Cassidy moved and scooped up her cat in her arms. "Did you hear that, Sir Whiskers? I'm not going to jail, which means you don't have to live with Aunt Petunia after all." Mr. Whiskers meowed in relief.

Chapter 17

Diane called me after I left Cassidy's shop. "You have to see this," she said before I could even say hello.

"See what?"

"Roger reminded me that we paid for cloud storage for our security system. The company backs up our surveillance data for thirty days. It's all right here."

"What's there?"

"Mr. Haggerty, he came into the bakery Saturday morning around seven thirty. He placed his order and then went into the restroom. Amber then came in with that new deputy. She placed an order but then got distracted chatting with the deputy. Get this, Amber took Mr. Haggerty's drink and left. Then, when Mr. Haggerty came out, he motioned to Amber's drink as if asking if it was his.

Anna comes into the frame, nods, and tells Mr. Haggerty to " have a good day."

"Wait, are you saying that Amber was the intended target?"

"I think so. I mean, if he was poisoned at the bakery, how else would you explain it?" Diane asked.

"Unless someone slipped the potion into his drink between the bakery and the inn?"

"I suppose that's possible, and it would clear my staff's names."

"Can you see who made the drinks?"

"No, the machine's not in the frame. The camera is more for watching the register."

"Where's Anna now? And what did you say the other worker's name was?" I only knew him by face.

"Kellan Mahoney."

"Where are they now?"

"I don't know. They both have the day off."

"Okay, I'm going to call the sheriff's department and fill them in. Cassidy also told me more about Mr. Haggerty. It turns out he had an incurable condition. It was getting progressively worse."

"No. Now I feel even more sorry for him."

"I know. Me too. He was seeing her to try and cure him."

"Given his review, I take it the medicine wasn't working."

"You'd be correct."

'That's too bad."

"I know. Let me make that call and update the sheriff about the drinks. Someone needs to question Anna and Kellan as soon as possible." I wasn't sure if the sheriff or Amber would listen. They didn't like when I uncovered evidence before them.

"Okay, and what do you want me to do?"

"Nothing, just stay where you are. I'll come to you."

I called the sheriff's department as I got in my car. "Hey, Dottie, is the sheriff available?"

"Oh, I'm afraid not."

"What about Deputy Reynolds?" I thought I should practice referring to Amber by her title if I was going to get on her good side. I wanted her listen to me for once and take the treat seriously.

"You must not have heard. There's been an accident."

"What kind of accident?" I stopped in the middle of buckling my seatbelt. I remembered hearing the sirens and wondered if they were connected.

"A bad one. We're all praying Deputy Reynolds will be alright."

"What happened?"

"It's just so awful. She lost control driving around the lake. Her cruiser hit a tree halfway down the bank."

"What? Is she okay?" The terrain on the other side of the lake was quite steep.

"I don't know. Her car didn't land in the lake, but it's not good."

"No, it doesn't sound like it. I'm sorry to hear that. Is Deputy Jones available?" I needed to tell someone about the swapped drinks.

"Hold on. He just got back from the scene; let me transfer you to him."

I waited for Deputy Jones to pick up the line.

"Deputy Jones," he said.

"Hey, it's Angelica. I have to talk to you about something." I went on to recap everything I knew about Mr. Haggerty's murder and how I suspected Amber was the target. "What do you think?"

"I think you're right. The preliminary investigation shows Amber's brake lines were cut."

I swallowed uncomfortably. Now, more than ever, I was convinced she had been the target all along.

"You need to find Anna and Kellan and bring them in for questioning." I didn't mean to tell the deputy how to do his job, but I couldn't help it.

"Agree. I'm on it right now."

"How's Amber doing? Do you know anything?"

"No, the sheriff is at the hospital. Amber was unconscious last I knew."

"Okay, I'm going to head up there. Diane has

the camera footage on her phone. I want to show it to the sheriff and see what he thinks."

"Tell him I'll be in touch."

"Will do."

Thirty minutes later, I managed to do just that. Vance and Diane met me in the waiting room with Sheriff Reynolds. The cozy space offered some privacy. "I don't know what to think about all of this," the sheriff sat down, stood up, and sat back down again. He had already watched the video ten times.

"Does Amber have any enemies?" I asked the sheriff. I meant besides me, and I didn't count. I might not like Amber, but I never wanted to see her hurt. Have her grow up a little bit? Maybe. Become a better person? Most definitely. But get hurt? Never.

"I don't know. She's a good deputy; she's put away a lot of bad guys." There was no question that the sheriff thought highly of his daughter.

"Has anyone recently been paroled?" Vance asked.

"I don't know." The sheriff looked down at his folded hands in his lap.

"Or what about convictions overturned?" I remember seeing that two of Amber's convictions had been thrown out over the last year. That meant we knew of at least two individuals who might want to seek revenge.

"I don't know." The sheriff shook his head. Those three words seemed to be the only thing the sheriff could say.

Vance turned his attention to Diane. "What are your staff's full names?"

"Anna Sanderson and Kellan Mahoney."

Vance turned to the sheriff. "What about those two surnames? Do they ring any bells?" The sheriff zoned out and continued to stare at the floor. Diane, Vance, and I shared a look. We weren't getting anywhere here. The sheriff was too shocked to answer.

"Well, hopefully, Deputy Jones can track them down and find out which one made Amber's drink and what they had against Amber," I said.

"I agree. Maybe this nightmare will be over sooner rather than later."

"Is there anything we can get you, Sheriff?" I asked.

"No, I'm fine. I'll be here if anyone needs me. I'm not leaving until I know how my baby girl's doing."

"Go, I'll stay with him," Diane offered.

Vance and I turned to walk away, but the sheriff stopped us. "Normally, I'd be mad at you for doing my job, but right now, I'm numb. Can't promise I won't chew you out tomorrow."

I smiled. "I look forward to it."

My phone chimed in my pocket. It was Deputy Jones calling me. "Are you still with the sheriff?"

"Yes, he's right here."

"Tell him to give me a call."

I turned away from the sheriff. "He's in a bit of shock at the moment. I'm not sure if it's the best time."

"It's that barista of Diane's, Kellan Mahoney?"

"Yeah?"

"We just found him. He's dead."

I was sure that my mouth was left wide open.

"What? What is it?" Vance looked at me with a concerned expression.

"Kellan is dead," I wasn't sure why I was whispering. Perhaps it was the sacred nature of the hospital waiting room. I didn't want to bring any negativity into a space that was already filled with such tension. Or maybe it was because I didn't know how to break the news to Diane. Kellan had been working for her for some time. Blurting out that he was dead wasn't the right way to go about it.

"Angelica? Can you hear me?" Deputy Jones asked. "Can you tell the sheriff? He's going to want to know."

"Yeah, I'll let them know."

"I can handle the investigation, but I want him to be aware. Tell him to call me when he can."

"I will. Anything else?"

Deputy Jones seemed like he was weighing his options. Finally, he must've realized there was no sense in keeping any information from me. "Tell him it was a suicide. We have a note, and it looks like he used the same potion that killed Mr. Haggerty."

"Final Night potion?"

"How did you figure that out? The department hasn't released that information."

"Connie helped me analyze it." It paid to be friends with a potion expert.

"Of course she did."

I walked farther away from the group. "So what? Kellan accidentally killed Mr. Haggerty and then tried to kill Amber?"

"His note doesn't say anything about Mr. Haggerty, only Amber. He said she had to pay for her crimes."

"What crimes?"

"We're still piecing it together, but he thinks he killed her."

"He thought he killed Amber and then went and killed himself? What, out of guilt?"

"Sounds like it."

I frowned. "There has to be more to it. What's his connection to Amber?"

"Still working on it. Hang on." The deputy shouted something to another member of the team. They continued to have a side conversation. "Listen, I'm pretty busy here."

"Sorry, I know you are. I'll relay all the information."

I turned hesitantly back to Sheriff Reynolds and Diane. Diane met my eyes. "There's been a break in the case?" she asked.

"Something like that."

Diane frowned.

I pressed on. "That was Deputy Jones. They're at Kellan's house, and Kellan's passed away."

The sheriff snapped his head up. "Did he say how?"

"He drank the Final Night potion." I let the implications hang in the air.

"No." Diane covered her mouth in shock. "You mean he killed Mr. Haggerty and started the fire? I can't believe that. Kellan wouldn't do that."

"I guess there's a note. Deputy Jones says it doesn't mention Mr. Haggerty, but he does confess to going after Amber. According to the note, he thinks he killed her."

The sheriff growled. I took a step back. "Why did he want to murder my daughter?"

"Something about paying for her crimes. If you want to go, we can stay here, and you can meet Deputy Jones," I offered.

The sheriff looked torn.

I looked over at Diane. "Is Amber stable right now?"

Diane shrugged her shoulder. "I don't know."

The sheriff answered. "She's in surgery. The doctor said the seatbelt ruptured her spleen, and she has a broken hip. I don't want to leave just yet."

"Okay, we'll keep working the case then. If you need me to do anything, just let Diane know, and she'll get ahold of me," I offered. Sheriff Reynolds wasn't one to ask for my help, but this was his daughter we were talking about. He might like to give me grief, but I had to believe that deep down inside, he knew I was good at solving mysteries, and if you asked me, this case was far from being solved.

Again, we turned to leave.

"Angelica?" The sheriff's voice stopped me once more.

"Yeah?"

"If you two are going to keep investigating this, I'm officially deputizing you."

I looked back at Vance. Was the sheriff serious? By the look on his face, he was.

"Both of us?" I asked.

"Seems only right," the sheriff replied.

"You don't think it's a simple case of Kellan having it out for your daughter?" Vance asked.

"No," was his one-word response. I had to agree with him. "I'll let Jones know. I expect you to work together," he added.

"Um, yes … sir." I stumbled over my words, unsure of what being deputized fully entailed and how this changed my relationship with the sheriff.

Sheriff Reynolds took out his phone and made a call. I could tell it was to Deputy Jones, given the conversation. There was no need for us to wait around.

Diane held her pinkie and thumb in the universal "call me" sign. I nodded that I would, and Vance and I left.

Chapter 18

Vance and I left the hospital and walked back to our cars. I knew the town picnic was in full swing, but now wasn't the time to celebrate.

"That was unexpected," I confessed.

"It just shows you how much the sheriff respects us."

"And how concerned he is for his daughter."

Vance and I stood in the parking lot between our cars. "You know, nothing about this case adds up. There are still too many holes," I said.

"I agree."

"I'm glad it's not just me. Maybe it would make more sense if we knew how Kellan tied in with Amber. He had to have a personal vendetta."

"The part that doesn't make sense the most is, even if we do figure out the connection, why did he kill himself? He wasn't even a person of interest."

"Maybe he figured it was only a matter of time before the case led to him?" I suggested.

"Maybe, but it seems a bit premature."

"That's not the only thing that seems premature," I added.

"You mean because he assumed he killed Amber?"

"Right. He first tries to poison her coffee and when that doesn't work, cuts her break lines and just assumes it works?"

"Her car was totaled," Vance pointed out.

"I know, but wouldn't you wait to see if you were successful? I mean, if that was your goal?"

"You're right. The timing doesn't add up." Vance looked off into the distance. A telltale sign he was deep in thought. "I'd like to find out more about what was in his note. You would think that Kellan would have at least mentioned Mr. Haggerty."

"You would think, especially if that contributed to his guilt and why he killed himself," I said.

"Unless he was so determined to seek revenge, he didn't care who he killed in the process?"

"I don't know. I can't get my head around the fact that Kellan, the twenty-something barista at Diane's bakery, is behind all of this. I don't see it. I know Diane doesn't see it either. I asked her earlier before we had the footage."

"I'm going to say this case is not closed."

"No, most definitely not."

"What do you say we get some Chinese food and head back to my place? We can dive into Kellan's background and try to link him with Amber and lay everything out. We have to be missing something."

"You're right. We have to be. I think it sounds like a plan."

Diane called me two hours later. Vance and I had turned his dining room into investigation head-quarters. "We're home now. The doctors released Roger after his test came back normal. He's going to have to take it easy for a bit, but other than that, everything's okay."

"That's wonderful news. I was going to call you in a little bit. Vance and I are trying to piece the case together, and it just doesn't make sense with Kellan as the killer. I mean, you knew him the most. I know I asked you earlier, but can you see it?"

"To be honest, I can't. He seemed like a good kid. He was a bit down on his luck lately, money troubles from what I understood, but instead of complaining about it, he asked to pick up more hours. I never had any problems with him calling off or not showing up. The whole case baffles me. I mean, he waited on Amber almost every morning. Why would he snap now? I don't get it."

"Yeah, that's what Vance and I are thinking. I'm not sure how he fits in if he's an accomplice or scapegoat, but I don't see him as the mastermind here."

"I've got something," Vance said. He had been typing on his keyboard, searching all the databases to find out information on Kellan.

"Deputy Jones just emailed this to both of us. Facial recognition pulled up a hit. Only his name isn't Kellan Mahoney. It's Troy Darvin. He did three years in Jacksonville for carjacking."

"I stand corrected."

"What? What did Vance say?" Diane asked.

"Did you know Kellan's real name was Troy, and he did prison time?"

"What? Are you sure?"

I moved to stand behind Vance and read over his shoulder. "I'm looking at his mug shot right now. It's definitely Kellan, although he looks a bit younger. I'd say a teenager."

"He was sentenced to eight years but only did three. Not sure why yet," Vance said as he continued scrolling.

My other line clicked in. It was Deputy Jones. "Hang on, Diane. Deputy Jones is calling me."

I put Diane's line on hold and answered the second call.

"I heard you're one of us now," Deputy Jones said.

"I'm not even sure what that means."

"It means the sheriff is not messing around, and

he wants all hands on deck solving this case. It also means I can share information with you."

When Deputy Jones explained it that way, it didn't sound like such a bad deal. "I just emailed you a mugshot of Kellan, his real name was Troy Darvin. I don't see a link between him and Amber other than he's on the other side of the law. I thought maybe you wanted to try to work that angle. We have a lead on the sapphire that I'm trying to track down. The cases might be connected," the deputy remarked.

"Okay, we'll keep working and let you know what we come up with."

"There's more," Deputy Jones added before I could hang up.

"More?"

"Dr. Humphrey put Troy's time of death at some time yesterday. At least twenty-four hours ago."

"Not today."

"No. He didn't cut Amber's brakes."

"So he was a scapegoat."

"Possibly. I'm still not sure how it all pieces together."

"Okay, let me see what we can uncover."

I hung up with the deputy and clicked back over to Diane, putting the call on speaker so I could fill her and Vance in together.

"We were right about things not adding up. Dr.

Humphrey says that Troy, a.k.a. Kellen died some-time yesterday. At least twenty-four hours ago."

"So what does that mean?" Diane asked. "Do you need me to meet you?"

"No, stay home and take care of Roger. Vance and I will figure out who set Kellan up."

"It could have been an accomplice that turned on him," Vance mentioned.

"That's probably more like it," I agreed.

"Do you know if a deputy talked to Anna?" I asked Diane. The second barista was as sweet as possible, but I wasn't leaving any stone unturned.

"No, but I talked to her. She called me when she heard about Kellan. She was at her grandmother's eightieth birthday. She doesn't know anything about a poisoned latte. She said she didn't go anywhere near Amber or Mr. Haggerty's drinks. She was in the back, making cupcakes for her grandmother."

"And you believe her?" Vance asked.

"I do. She's so upset. I guess Kellan had recently asked her out, and they had grown a bit close since he picked up more hours through the summer."

"Would it be okay if I talked to her?" I asked. If she was close to Kellan, she might know more than she realized.

"I don't see why not. Let me send you her contact information. I'll let her know you might be calling."

"Okay, thanks. If you hear of anything else, call me immediately." I hung up with Diane and sighed.

"How do you want to do this?" Vance asked.

"I think I should talk to Anna, and you keep trying to figure out how Kellan fits in. What do you think?"

"That's as good a plan as we have. From what I can tell, looking at his record, Amber didn't put him in jail. His arrest and conviction all happened in Florida."

"Nothing to do with Silverlake whatsoever?"

"Nothing," Vance continued reading his screen.

"So why get involved?"

"Maybe he was being paid? Diane said he had some money troubles."

"You mean he could be like a hired hitman?"

"It's one option."

"I wonder if Deputy Jones found any cash in Kellan's house." Instead of wondering, I went ahead and called the deputy back and put my cell phone on speaker. "Hey, did you find any money on Kellan? Vance and I are wondering if he was a hired hit man."

"No, I haven't found anything of value yet, but that's not a bad theory."

"Does he have a safe in the closet or something?"

"Not that we've found, but we're just getting started here. If I find something, I'll let you know."

"Thanks, appreciate it." I clicked off with Deputy Jones and looked to Vance.

"If somebody paid you money and you wanted to hide it, where would you put it?" he asked.

"I'd probably hide it somewhere in my house unless I didn't think it was safe."

"I wouldn't put it in the bank," Vance thought.

"No, bank deposits can be traced, but what about a safe-deposit box?" Silverlake had only one bank in town. It wouldn't be hard to stop in to see if Kellan had a safe-deposit box on my way to talk with Anna. I decided I wanted to speak to her in person. I found I could tell a lot about a person by not only what they said but how they acted. I wanted to get a visual read on the young woman. It took me a minute to remember that it was Sunday, and the bank was closed. The day was slipping away. We'd completely skipped the town picnic, and it would be too late to do much of anything soon. And did I really want to crash Anna's grandmother's eightieth birthday?"

"What's wrong?" Vance asked.

"Hmm?"

"You're frowning."

"I was just thinking that maybe instead of running here and there chasing down leads, I need to sit and think for a minute."

"That's not a bad idea."

"I feel like I'm missing something in plain sight.

Let me think here." I left the kitchen table and moseyed into the living room to sit in the quiet for a minute.

IT TURNED out that sitting and thinking for a few moments translated into me falling asleep on Vance's couch and taking a nap. That was unexpected.

When I woke, it was just before nine o'clock. I heard the shower running upstairs, so I knew Vance was taking a research break.

At least I didn't have to feel bad about skipping out on interviewing Anna because when I checked my phone, I saw that she had tried to get ahold of me.

After getting a drink of water, I sat comfortably back on the couch, tucked a blanket around my waist, and gave Anna a callback. "Sorry, I know it's getting late, but I just saw that you called," I explained when she picked up the line.

"No, that's all right. I'm glad you got back to me tonight. I've been thinking about Kellan, and I might know some things to help the case." My ears perked up at that. "Is now a good time to talk?"

"Yeah." I cleared the remaining sleep from my voice. "Right now is great."

I could hear Anna take a deep breath on the

other end. "The thing is, Kellan did some time in prison. Diane never knew about it, and he made me promise I would never tell her."

I tried not to be disappointed, but Anna wasn't telling me anything I already didn't know. "We found out about his prison stint a little bit ago," I confessed.

"You did?"

"Uh-huh. We know Kellan Mahoney was a fake name. Kellan's real name was Troy Darvin."

"I knew that, too. Kellan told me he changed his identity for protection. He never told me who he was hiding from, only that he came to Silverlake to start over. He thought he would be safe here."

"He never said why he was hiding?"

Anna was quiet; I felt she knew more than she let on. "I get that you're scared."

"They're not my secrets to tell, and what if they come after me too?"

I wanted to promise Anna that I would protect her, but I couldn't make that promise until I knew who she was hiding from. Even if she told me, I couldn't guarantee her safety. I was just one witch with magical abilities that occasionally went haywire. "I understand keeping quiet, but if you decide you want to tell me more, I'm here."

Anna seemed to have an internal struggle, but then she said, "I am pretty good with protection charms. I offered one to Kellan, but he thought he didn't need one."

"You did all that you could." I didn't want Anna beating herself up over Kellan's death. He was obviously involved in something he shouldn't have been.

"What I mean is that I can protect myself." Something about the strength in Anna's voice made me long to have that much confidence in my magical abilities. "He snitched on someone in prison. That's how he got out early. Once out, he decided to make a new life for himself, and I thought he was on his way until a week ago."

"What happened a week ago?"

"I don't know. He seemed jumpy, on edge. He was always laughing and joking around with me, and then he flat out stopped. I could tell something was on his mind, but he didn't want to talk to me about it, and I didn't push. I wish I had now."

"Please, don't blame yourself."

"I'm not. I know it's not my fault, even if it feels that way. I'm not sure what happened, but I can't believe Kellan tried to kill Amber. If he poisoned that latte, it wasn't because he wanted to."

"You think he was coerced?"

"He would've had to have been. The Kellan I knew wasn't a murderer. He wouldn't have taken his own life, either. He worked hard to start over. He was excited about the future. We talked about traveling together. Both of us wanted to see the world."

Anna's voice grew strained, and I could tell she was crying.

"I'm sorry that he's gone."

Anna caught her breath. "I hope you can find out what happened."

"I know. So do I."

Chapter 19

"Where are we at with this case?" Clemmie's phone call woke me up bright and early Monday morning at seven o'clock. It took me a minute to get my brain working and formulate a response.

"Hello? You there?" Clemmie asked.

"Sorry, I haven't had any coffee yet."

"Best I can do is some black tea. You want me to send a cup your way?" I made a face. "Don't make that face."

I pulled the phone away from my ear and looked at the screen. We weren't on a video call, so I had no idea how Clemmie knew I had pulled a face.

"Because I know you and how much you like your morning coffee. That's how I know," Clemmie responded to my unasked question. "Anyway, I've got news. You ready for this?"

"Ready."

"I heard our boy Kellan had done time. So I started asking around. You know, we've had a lot of new folks move into town. It turns out Kellan wasn't the only one with a criminal history."

"There's someone else?"

"You're never going to believe this, but it's Terry Dawes."

"Oh, no, I believe that, all right. Do you know when he went to jail and what for?"

"No, and no. I just know he told Craig Daniels that he did a stint in the slammer and was wondering if Craig was related to a Kirk Daniels. It was a buddy he knew on the inside."

"Interesting. Is Craig related to that other guy?"

"Not that he knew of."

"Huh. I wonder if Terry is somehow connected to Kellan?"

"That sounds like a Vance question," Clemmie remarked. She was right. Vance was the one good with research. No one knew the criminal justice information system like he did. "I don't want you or Misty going and talking with Terry, either, you hear?"

"Speaking of Misty, I didn't see her all day yesterday, did you?"

"No, ma'am. I was too busy winning the chili cook-off."

"You did? Congratulations."

"I'd ask where you were, but I know you've been running yourself ragged trying to solve this case."

"That I am. Hey, how did Luke do?"

"Second place. He gave me a run for my money, but no one can resist Ms. Clemmie's chili once they have a taste. It's that good."

"I bet."

"Promise me you won't go talk to Terry," Clemmie brought the conversation back on track.

"You don't have to tell me twice."

"Good, be sure to let me know if there's anything I can do on my end."

"You know I will. I'll talk to you soon, okay?"

"You got it."

Now that I was awake for the morning, I decided I should get ready and head to the bank. Before leaving, I called Misty. She didn't answer her cell phone, so I called up to the bookstore.

"Hey Vicki, I was wondering if Misty was working today?"

"No, she called in for the day."

"She did? Is everything okay?"

"Define okay."

"Oh no, does this have anything to do with Daniel?"

"You mean that low-life, ridiculous rock star who wasted her time and broke her heart?"

I guess that answered that question. "He broke up with her?"

"I guess so. All I know is she asked me to cover for her yesterday and today. I'm hoping she comes in tomorrow because I could use a day off after the busy weekend."

"I don't blame you. I'll stop by and visit her in a little bit."

"Don't tell her I said anything."

"Don't worry. I won't."

I would've stopped by Misty's house first if I didn't think she might still be sleeping. Misty was a lot like me and didn't like waking up before nine o'clock and would sleep in later if she didn't have to be anywhere. Seeing she called in to work, I figured she might be getting extra rest.

The bank was busy, even for a Monday morning. From the look of the number of business owners in line making deposits, I had to assume the bicentennial weekend had been a success in terms of revenue. That put a smile on my face. I always liked seeing Silverlake succeed despite the recent unfortunate events. Mayor Parrish should be proud of herself for pulling off another successful event.

"Hey, Molly," I said to Mr. McCormick's daughter. "Pretty busy this morning, huh?"

"Mondays usually are, but today it's extra busy. I don't mind. It'll make the day go by faster. How was your weekend?" One of the things I liked about Molly was how upbeat and talkative she was, but not when I had some important sleuthing to do.

"My weekend was okay, but I wanted to ask you something. Did you hear about Kellan Mahoney."

"I did. Isn't that just awful? He was such a nice young man."

"Did he have a bank account here?"

"He sure did. He came in every week and deposited his check from the bakery."

I had to be careful what I told Molly because the woman could talk. Whatever I told her, she was sure to tell everyone else. "Does anything jump out as being odd about his account?"

"What do you mean?"

"Like, did he have an unusual amount of money or make a large deposit recently?"

"Oh, I'm sorry. I wish I could tell you, but that's private information."

I debated if I should tell Molly I was a deputy now. Once I told her, everyone would know. Then again, just because I was a deputy now didn't mean I had to remain one. For all I knew, the sheriff could revoke the right at any given moment.

Decisions, decisions.

I decided solving this case was worth the bit of gossip the deputy news would generate. "I cleared my throat. Good news, then. You can tell me. Sheriff Reynolds deputized me yesterday and asked me to personally investigate this case."

Molly's face lit up like a Christmas tree. "He did? My word, congratulations!" Everyone around the lobby looked at Molly to see what she was so excited about. "I always knew you'd make a good deputy. You're so smart. Remember how you used to help me study in high school? You always knew all those dates. I could never keep them straight."

I smiled uncomfortably at the unwanted attention.

"Plus all those other cases you've solved. The sheriff is lucky to have you!"

"What's going on now?" Mrs. Potts, my second-grade teacher, chimed in from the back of the line.

"Angelica is Silverlake's newest deputy!" Molly raised her voice and announced it for everyone to hear.

"That's great!" Honor from the charmery shouted.

"About time," Mrs. Potts added.

"Congrats, Angelica!" Lacy from the cloak shop exclaimed.

"Thanks, guys," I smiled before quickly turning back to Molly. "Now, about Kellan's bank records."

"Oh, right." Molly typed on her keyboard and clicked around on a few more screens before saying, "No, there's nothing here. I only see his regular paycheck. The withdrawals are for everyday things like the gas station and grocery store. Let me print it out for you."

"Okay, thanks." I couldn't help but feel like I'd let my deputy secret slip for nothing. Molly returned with the printout. "One more thing, did Kellan have a safe-deposit box?

"Let me check." Again, Molly clicked around on her keyboard. "I'm sorry, I don't see anything. There's not a box registered in his name."

"Well, shoot." I knew it was a long shot.

Molly leaned across the counter. "I heard he tried to kill Amber. Is that true?"

"We're still not sure." Again, I had to be careful with what I revealed. "But he might not have been working alone."

"Really? Do you think her ex is involved?"

"Whose ex? Amber's?"

"Uh-huh. She had a nasty breakup."

"With whom? I didn't know she was seeing anyone."

"Chip Ferguson."

"Dippy Chippy? The man that runs the ice cream cart?"

"That's him. He was devastated when Amber dumped him. He tried buying her roses, gave her jewelry, wrote her a song, and even named an ice cream flavor after her."

"That's impressive. What's it called?"

"Amber of My Eye."

"Amber of My Eye, is that like apple of my eye?

"Huh. I never thought of it that way. That would make sense because it's apple-flavored ice cream with caramel swirls. Isn't that the most romantic thing you've ever heard?"

"It's certainly the most creative."

"But nothing worked."

"She wouldn't take him back, huh?"

"No, and he was so heartbroken, but lately? I don't know. It's like he's changed. He put a layer of ice cream right around that heart of his. It's a shame because he used to be so nice."

"I see. Thanks for letting me know." I turned to walk away.

"Hey, are you also helping to track down the sapphire?"

"Not officially. Why, have you heard something?"

"Just what my dad told me."

"What's that?"

"Did you know that they bewitched the sapphire so that it will drive you crazy if you steal it?"

"Wait, what? They cursed the sapphire?" Is that what my aunt meant by added protection? So much for it being top secret. If Molly knew, so did half the town.

"It's not really a curse, just a spell. My dad said that the sapphire wouldn't do anything to you if you had good intentions. But if you're up to no good? It would eat away at your conscience and drive you crazy until you get rid of it."

"Yikes. It was smart thinking on the council's part."

"I thought so. Although, I told my dad it would be smarter if they told everyone about it. Maybe no one would've stolen it in the first place if they had known it would make them go nuts."

"Good point." And something to think about in the future. That is, if we ever found it.

Chapter 20

After leaving the bank, I called Vance. "Hey, have you seen Dippy anywhere this morning?"

"Chippy Dippy?"

"That's the one."

"Um, no?"

"Molly at the bank told me he had been dating Amber. Did you know that?"

"I did not."

"It sounds like they had a rough breakup."

"Rough enough for him to want to kill her?"

"I don't know. Dippy always seems a bit odd to me. I guess I wouldn't be completely shocked if he went off the deep end."

"I wouldn't either."

"Do you want to do a background check on him, and I'll see if I can track him down?"

"Okay, but be careful. Don't go down any dark alleys with him and the ice cream cart."

"Don't worry. I won't. I've seen enough horror films to know when I should run in the opposite direction."

"Well, that's a relief," Vance chuckled.

"Oh, there was one other thing. I can't believe I didn't tell you this first. I must have too much information swirling in my brain. Clemmie called me this morning. Guess who else has a prison record. Terry Dawes."

"That's not surprising."

"That's what I said. Do you want to see if he has a connection to Kellan?"

"I'll see what I can find. Right now, I have a call in to a friend in Jacksonville. Trying to see what he can tell me about Kellan and who he ratted out."

"Let me know if you find anything out about Kellan or Dippy. I'll catch up with you in a little bit."

"Sounds good."

But before I could track down Dippy, I had to pay my best friend a visit.

I knocked on Misty's front door and patiently waited for her to answer. The house was quiet, and her blinds were shut, but her car was there.

"Misty? I can see your car in the garage. I know your home, and Vicki told me you called in. Hurry up and answer the door so I know you're okay."

After a moment, I heard the dead bolt slide back, and Misty opened her door. I have never seen my best friend look so disheveled. She hadn't brushed her hair. She had no makeup on. And she was wearing a dirty T-shirt and a pair of pajama pants.

"Happy now?" she replied dryly.

"No. What is going on? Are you sick?" I knew Vicki said Misty was nursing a broken heart, but maybe she was wrong.

"No, I'm not sick. I'm depressed." Misty walked away from the door and implied for me to follow her.

"Is it because of Daniel?"

"Don't even say his name." Misty plopped on the couch and pulled a blanket over her head. "I feel like such an idiot." Her muffled voice came through the fleece.

"Did he actually break up with you?"

"No, but does it matter? He's going to."

"Misty, listen to yourself. If it were me acting like this, you would lecture me up one side and down the other. You would tell me to quit being ridiculous, call my boyfriend, and make sure everything was okay."

"I can't. I know he will break up with me, and I already feel awful. I just can't deal with it right now."

"All because of one prediction?"

"I don't know."

"I think you do."

I gave Misty a moment to think.

"No, I guess it's not just one prediction. How am I supposed to compete with him and his lifestyle? Do you know how many fans are obsessed with him? Women throw themselves at him all the time. It was fun and exciting at first, but now, I don't know. I'm not a rock-star, party girl. I hate to say it, but I want to settle down and plant roots and all the things I never thought I wanted. But I do want it, and if I'm being honest, I want it with Daniel."

"But?"

"But I don't think he wants it with me. I don't know anymore."

I sat back in the chair, pleased that Misty was finally being honest with herself. All Amelia's prediction did was give her the catalyst to re-examine her feelings.

"Okay, that may be true, but I think you're doing Daniel and your relationship with him a disservice by running away from him. You're better than that. Stronger than that. Nobody likes having tough conversations, but you've never run away from them before."

Misty flopped the blanket off of her head. "Since when did you become so smart?"

"Since my best friend made me examine my feelings and reconnect with Vance, remember? It's not easy being honest with yourself, but the alternative is far worse."

"So now, what do I do?"

"Talk to Daniel."

"And if I'm not ready for that?"

"Stop being such a downer, and let's go do something fun."

"Like what?"

"Like catch a killer."

Misty and I found Dippy pushing his ice cream cart around the high school parking lot. "Hey, Dippy, what's going on?"

The sandy-haired and freckle-faced man looked down at his fitness tracker. "Nine thousand nine hundred and ninety-seven, nine thousand nine hundred and ninety-eight, nine thousand nine hundred and ninety-nine, ten thousand. Whew! A new afternoon record. Getting my steps in between lunch hours." Dippy was wearing a white button-up shirt tucked into a pair of pressed khakis. A red bow tie and pair of sneakers completed his look.

"Wow, that's great, Dippy," I remarked.

"Yeah, good job," Misty added, giving me a strange look.

"And pushing the ice cream cart, too. That has to count extra," I added.

"That's what I said, but my tracker doesn't have an ice cream cart accessory. No matter how often I email the manufacturer and request it as an added feature, they just won't do it."

Neither Misty nor I knew what to say to that.

Thankfully, Dippy pressed on. "What can I get for you guys? This week's feature is Bicentennial Blueberry. I still have quite a bit left over from the weekend."

"Oh, no ice cream for me," I said.

"I'm good," Misty added.

"No ice cream?" Dippy looked confused.

"Afraid not. I was wondering if you had a minute to talk about Amber."

"Why, what have you heard? Did she tell you to come talk to me?" Dippy's face immediately lit up.

"Not exactly."

His expression shifted from joy to sorrow. "Oh, figures. I thought she would come to her senses by now. I'm quite the catch, you know." Dippy cocked his head in admiration.

I couldn't fault his self-esteem, but that led me to think of something else. If Dippy thought Amber sent us, then he didn't know she was injured.

"When's the last time you spoke to Amber?" I asked.

"Saturday. She told me that if I didn't quit threatening her, she would have me arrested," Dippy nodded.

"And why were you threatening her?" Misty asked.

"I wasn't! I tried telling her it wasn't me, but she didn't believe me."

Misty and I shared a look. "Did Amber say how you were threatening her?" I asked.

"She said something about a creepy note but didn't go into details. Would you tell her it wasn't me if you talk to her? I really don't want to get arrested."

There was no easy way to tell Dippy about Amber, but he had to know. I needed to break the news gently. "I can try to tell her, but the thing is, Amber was in an accident."

All the blood drained from Dippy's face. "Accident?" At least, I think that's what he said. His mouth formed the word accident, but hardly any sound came out. "Is she okay? Where is she? I have to go to her. She might need my help." Dippy left the ice cream cart in the middle of the parking lot and started power walking away from it.

"Dippy, hang on!" Misty and I jogged to catch up. "Amber's at the hospital. The accident happened yesterday. She's already out of surgery and resting. The sheriff is with her."

"I don't care who's with her. I need to see her. Until then, I won't be able to calm down. Watch my cart for me, will you?"

"Um, is there someplace we can store it?" I asked.

"Take it to the cafeteria. Ask Mrs. Mueller if she

can store it in the freezer," Dippy said as he continued to power walk away from us.

"You said this was going to be fun," Misty said as she started to push the ice cream cart toward the sidewalk.

"What do you mean? This is fun. Look, I got you free ice cream." Misty looked at me like I was just as nutty as Dippy. "Come on. There might even be waffle cones."

Chapter 21

We tucked the ice cream cart safely inside the walk-in freezer at the high school. "You know, I think we should probably follow Dippy and head to the hospital. If Amber is awake, she might be able to tell us more about this creepy note of hers and give us some clue as to who's been harassing her."

"You make a good point. Maybe she also knows why Kellan was the one to carry out the poisoning."

"And she might not have been responsible for Kellan's arrest, but she could be responsible for Terry's."

"What about Terry now?"

"Sorry, I left that part out. He also has a criminal record. Clemmie called and told me about it this morning."

"So you think maybe Kellan and Terry are working together?"

"It was one theory. I was also curious about Dippy, but he obviously didn't do anything to harm her."

"No way. That man is definitely nursing some big feelings for Deputy Reynolds."

"Do you want to head to the hospital with me?"

"Do you need me to?" Misty still looked a little rough.

"No, I guess not. Want me to take you home?"

"Do you mind taking me to Village Square? I haven't been to the bookshop in a couple of days, and I should pop in and check on things. After that, I'll head home and call Daniel."

"You will?"

"You are right. I've been an idiot. Dippy made me realize I shouldn't throw everything away just because of one psychic reading. I care for Daniel just like how he cares for Amber. Sometimes you have to fight for those you love."

"Good for you. I'll take you to the bookstore right this minute."

With most tourists back home, traffic was light, and we made it back around the lake in record time. I had planned to drop Misty off in the parking lot until she said, "Oh before I forget, your aunt's new romance novel came in. Do you mind coming in and grabbing it quickly? She had put a rush order on it. Something about just having to know how a series ends."

"Sure, I can run in." There was nothing worse than waiting for the next book in a series.

"Great. She tried conjuring it, but it was sold out everywhere." Misty opened the door, and I followed her inside. "Daniel! What are you doing here?" Misty stopped in her tracks. I hadn't been paying attention. I had been looking at the new front display featuring five-minute spells and almost walked right into her.

"There you are!" Daniel had a broad grin. In three strides, he stood before Misty and scooped her up in a big hug. "I've been looking everywhere for you. I would have called your phone, but I wanted it to be a surprise."

My friend was speechless.

"Is everything okay?" Daniel seemed unsure.

"I'm shocked. I wasn't expecting you until next week."

"I missed you, and I thought maybe you might miss me too."

I had to stop myself from gushing over how adorable the two of them were. I liked to think that Amelia was a gifted psychic, but there were some things that even professionals could get wrong, like my best friend's relationship status.

"Here, I got you something." Daniel took Misty by the hand and led her to the counter, where a gift bag was waiting.

Vicki took it as her cue to duck out from behind

the counter. She walked around and passed me, whispering, "I thought they broke up?"

"I'll explain everything later. Do you by chance, have Aunt Thelma's book? It's a romance novel she rush-ordered?"

"Sure, let me go in the back and get it."

"You couldn't come on the tour, so I brought the tour to you. There's a pastry from Prague, some chocolates from Germany, a bottle of wine from Italy," Daniel said each item as Misty took them out of the bag.

The last item was a small parcel wrapped in tissue paper. "I met the most talented stained glass artist in Austria," Daniel explained as Misty unwrapped it. "Oh man, don't tell me it broke."

Misty looked at the broken artwork in her hand and held it up for me to see. It had been in the shape of a heart. "A broken heart," she said more to me than Daniel.

I shook my head.

"I'm sorry. I'll have to reach out to the artist and see if I can get a new one sent." Misty chuckled to herself and then sighed. "What, what's so funny?"

"I'll tell you about it later. Right now, I'm just happy to have you home."

"Here's that book," Vicki said, passing the hardcover to me.

"Thank you. I'm going to run. Tell Misty I said

bye." I motioned with my head to where the couple was embracing.

Vicki smiled. "You got it. Have a good day."

"Thanks, you too."

When I got to the hospital, Sheriff Reynolds and Dippy were talking with one of Amber's doctors in the waiting room. I popped my head in to ask how she was doing. Upon seeing me, the sheriff interrupted the doctor, "Excuse me one moment." He turned his attention to me. "Do you have an update?" I knew what he meant. He wanted to see if I had a break in the case.

"Maybe. Is Amber awake?"

"She should be."

"Mind if I talk to her?"

"Go right ahead."

"Thanks."

As I walked to Amber's room, I tried to think about what I needed to ask her. I hoped she had kept the threatening note or any other evidence we could use to track down who was stalking her. Maybe stalking wasn't the right word. I wasn't sure if there was a word for multiple attempts of murder. I was surprised to see that Deputy Lopez wasn't outside Amber's door anymore, given how active the threat still was.

I pushed open the wooden door, and I was about to knock as I entered to announce my arrival, when I heard someone talking. I first thought it was a nurse or a doctor, seeing they drew the bedside curtain for privacy.

I stepped back, not wanting to eavesdrop, then the person's words reached my ears. "I don't get it. Why won't you die?" the voice asked. The words sent chills up my spine. My body froze, but my mind raced to figure out who was talking. I recognized the voice but couldn't put it with a face. It wasn't someone that I knew very well. "You destroy people's lives. My brother was innocent. He didn't deserve to go to jail. You ruined his life and my mother's. She died thinking my brother was a criminal. You didn't just break my brother; you broke my whole family."

Amber seemed to struggle with the right words. It wasn't until I heard her make a choking sound that I realized she wasn't struggling over what to say but to breathe.

I jumped into action, pulling the curtain back in time to see Deputy Lopez straddling Amber on the bed and choking her. I had never suspected the deputy of being the killer, and the realization that someone who was supposed to serve and protect could be capable of such violence was overwhelming. My hand moved on its own, reaching for my wand, pointing it at the deputy's chest, and shouting, "Stasi!" to stun her in place.

I belatedly remembered that the deputy was a shifter, and she had to be something strong; perhaps she had gargoyle blood somewhere down the line because the spell bounced off her. The only thing I managed to do was anger the crazed woman.

Deputy Lopez leaped off the bed and turned her rage toward me. Amber screamed. I pulled the bedside cart with Amber's lunch on it in front of me, using it as a shield. I wanted to put as much distance as possible between myself and the mad woman. That did little to detour the deputy.

Deputy Lopez charged. I could feel my heart racing in my chest. I was filled with a mixture of fear and anger. My mind was working quickly, trying to think of a way out of this situation. I was scared, but I was also determined to protect Amber and myself. I pushed the table toward her, grabbing whatever I could to throw at her along the way, which turned out to be a carton of sherbet and a cup of Jell-O. The sherbet hit the deputy on her shoulder and splattered melted orange goo across her face and hair. The Jell-O skidded across the hospital room floor along with a plate full of mashed potatoes and gravy.

"And you! Who are you?" the deputy growled. "You are always snooping around."

"I'm a witch who doesn't know when to back down." I stood my ground, trying to be the fearless witch I'd always wanted to be.

"UGH!" A flash of blue light came hurtling past my head. I almost didn't duck in time as the object cracked the room's mirror behind me and fell to the floor. I glanced down in time to see that it was the Silverlake Sapphire.

"That stupid rock. I thought it would buy me a new life, but all it's done is bring me problems. It's cursed, I tell you!"

"It's not cursed. It's bewitched to reflect your true colors," I shot back.

"What are you trying to say?"

"I think it's obvious."

"Everything I've done has been for my family." Deputy Lopez pointed at her chest.

"Is that what your brother would have wanted? What your mother would have wanted? For you to kill someone in revenge?"

"You don't know what it's like to watch the system that's supposed to protect people destroy your life. To hear someone lie just to close a case. That's what she did." The deputy stared at me but pointed her finger off to the side at Amber.

I couldn't wait for help to arrive. I had to act fast. I took a chance on the gargoyle theory and blasted Deputy Lopez with a sunlight spell. The entire room erupted in light. I blocked my eyes with my forearm, turning away. My hair blew back as I struggled to hold onto the wand. It was the one time when my overreacting powers paid off.

The light from the spell was intense, almost as if the sun had been brought down to earth. The white-hot rays seared through the room, illuminating every corner. Shadows were cast in every direction, and the room took on an otherworldly glow. Deputy Lopez was momentarily stunned by the sudden explosion of light. She stumbled back, her arms thrown up to shield her eyes. The orange goo from the sherbet melted away, and the Jell-O, mashed potatoes, and gravy were cast in sharp relief. For a moment, it was as if time stood still. And then, with a final burst of energy, the spell dissipated, leaving behind a room that was still in disarray but now a little brighter.

Deputy Lopez might not be a gargoyle, but the blinding light was enough to disorient her and gave me enough time to dash back to the room's door and scream for help.

I thought Sheriff Reynolds would be the first to arrive, but Dippy led the charge. The fearless ice cream man barreled down the hall. Once he realized Amber was okay and that it was Deputy Lopez I needed help taking down, he sprang into action. He was like a wild bull, charging right at her. Dippy wrapped his arms around Deputy Lopez's waist, and they crashed onto the ground and right on top of the rest of Amber's lunch. The two rolled in the smeared remnants of mashed potatoes and gravy.

The deputy rolled until Dippy was on his back. They moved so quickly that I couldn't get a clean shot with my wand. The alternative was that I could freeze them both, and I debated doing that when Dippy got the upper hand and somehow managed to roll over and sit on Deputy Lopez's back with her arms pinned behind her and her face smushed in gelatin.

"You will never lay a hand on her again, do you hear me?' Dippy commanded.

Both Amber and I were left speechless.

"She was strangling Amber when I walked in. Something about Amber ruining her brother's life," I explained to Sheriff Reynolds and the rest of the hospital staff who came to the rescue.

"He was innocent!" Deputy Lopez shrieked.

"Who's your brother?" Sheriff Reynolds asked.

"Nicky Oshay," Deputy Lopez growled.

"Stick Nicky?" Amber's voice was a whisper.

"Don't call him that! He made some bad choices, but he didn't rob that bank, and he didn't shoot the guard!"

"Bad choices? He was wanted in five other cases," Sheriff Reynolds replied.

"Pickpocketing cases. He didn't rob a bank!" Dippy struggled to remain in control of the deputy. She wiggled beneath him, but he held her arms firmly behind her back.

"Here, son, let me take over." Sheriff Reynold's clipped handcuffs onto the back of Deputy Lopez's wrists and began to read the deputy her rights as he escorted her out.

Amber struggled to sit up. Dippy ran to her side. His white shirt was stained with gravy. A fistful of mashed potatoes was stuck to his back. Amber didn't seem to mind. "You were amazing."

"I could never stand to see something bad happen to you. Despite what you think about me, I still love you," Dippy confessed.

"Oh, Dippy, I love you too!" Amber confessed.

"I think that's my cue to leave," I replied. I wasn't surprised when Amber and Dippy ignored me.

Vance called me as I walked out of the hospital. I was planning on calling him in a minute once I processed everything that had happened.

"Hey, we got a hit. I can't believe it, but Deputy Lopez's brother recently filed a lawsuit for false arrest and misconduct. The suit claims Amber misrepresented evidence in court, which led to his conviction."

"I know. The deputy went full psycho on Amber. The sheriff just arrested her."

"What?"

I filled Vance in on what had happened. "Hang on, Deputy Jones is calling me."

"You arrested Lopez?" he asked when I answered the phone.

"The sheriff should arrive with her at the station any minute."

"Good work, deputy."

"I'm not sure I'll ever get used to that." Not only that, but I had no intention of working down at the sheriff's department. I was already busy enough at the inn. I wondered if that was a prerequisite to the honor. Guess I'd have to wait and find out.

"I was on my way to question Deputy Lopez myself," Deputy Jones confessed.

"Oh yeah?"

"We got a call from a guy named Juan. He was Kellan's childhood best friend and the one guy he trusted. Kellan told him he was being blackmailed by Lopez. She knew he was in hiding. She threatened to blow his cover if he didn't poison Amber. When he said he still wouldn't do it, she said she would kill him."

"And he didn't go to the sheriff because?"

"Because as far as he was concerned, she was the sheriff."

"Let me ask you something. Deputy Lopez said her brother was innocent."

"Half brother," Deputy Jones clarified. "They had different fathers."

"That would explain the different last names."

"Mm-hmm, and why we didn't pick it up sooner."

"Do you think she's telling the truth? Was her brother innocent?"

"Deputies have a code. We don't talk bad about one another, but because you're one of us now, I don't mind telling you that, yeah, I think Amber messed up. Sticky Nicky did stupid things. He'd rob a candy store for a lollipop or lift a dollar out of your purse. When Amber fingered him for the robbery, I didn't think she was right. But it wasn't my case, and I didn't know the details. Looking back on it now, she was wrong."

"Do you think Amber will think twice before she accuses someone again?"

"She will if she's learned anything from all of this."

"If you were betting on it?"

"I'd say the odds are fifty-fifty."

"Yeah, I agree, but maybe she'll surprise us."

Chapter 22

I managed to get back to the inn later that evening with the Silverlake Sapphire safely in my possession. Maybe it was wrong of me to pocket it, but the fact that my conscious felt light and clear told me that my intentions had been pure. I only wanted the gemstone safely where it belonged.

When I walked in, Aunt Thelma sat with Amelia on the couch in the lobby. They had their eyes closed. Amelia's mother, Jane, sat across from them, sipping a mug of hot apple cider. Aunt Thelma loved to entertain, which was why I loved it when she was at home. She had goodies on the side table for guests to help themselves to almost every night. Tonight, there was a crockpot full of steaming apple cider and a tray of shortbread.

"Now, can you see a door?" Aunt Thelma asked.

"I can," Amelia confirmed.

"Good. Now, I want you to picture a screen door in front of it. Do you know what a screen door looks like?"

"Uh-huh. Like what we had at our old house."

Aunt Thelma cracked open an eye and looked at Jane, who nodded. "That's right. Now, the screen door lets some things through, but not everything. That's what we're going to do with your psychic visions. What do you think about that?"

"Okay. I'll try."

"Excellent. Remember that screen door? It's going to be rainbow colored.

"Oooh, I love rainbows."

"Perfect. Now, this rainbow screen will filter your visions so they are always happy and as pleasant as can be."

"I like the sound of that."

"I thought you would. All you have to do is repeat after me: Filter the dark. Let in the light. Show me the goodness and none of the fright."

Amelia repeated the spell after my aunt.

"Let's say it three times." I listened to my aunt and Amelia repeat the spell, locking it in place.

"Now, whatever visions you see will be happy. If you want to remove the spell, all you have to do is open the screen door and say: Show me everything that I can see. Hide no more. My vision is free."

"Don't worry. I'll write the counter spell down for your mom."

"Are you sure this will work?"

"It should, and if it doesn't, we will find the spell that does."

"Thank you, Ms. Nightingale. I appreciate it."

"As do I," Jane replied.

Watching the scene unfold, I couldn't help but wish I could filter everything in life through rose-colored glasses. Then again, maybe it was as simple as training your mind to focus on the positive. It was something to think about, especially as I looked toward the future. One thing I knew for sure was the world better watch out because I, Angelica Nightingale, was stepping into my power.

"Excuse me, is this the Mystic Inn?" A woman with short brown hair, wearing a disheveled business suit, and looking at bit ragged stood before me.

"Yes, ma'am. What can I do for you?"

"You can first tell me where I can find David Haggerty. He left me at the airport and told me we were headed to Silverlake, Iowa! Can you imagine? I have been all over the country looking for this little magical community of yours. What a nightmare. When I see that man, he is going to get it!"

"Let me guess, you're Catherine Kelly."

That stopped the woman in her tracks. "Why yes. You've heard of me?"

"Here, have a seat. I'll grab you some hot apple cider. You have a lot of catching up to do."

"Is that so?"

"It is. Welcome to Silverlake."

DON'T WORRY, the Silverlake adventures continue with Book 8: Jingle Bells & Wedding Spells

Stephanie Damore Complete Works
Mystic Inn Mysteries
Witchy Reservations
Eerie Check In
Spooked Solid
Untimely Departure
Midnight at Mystic Inn
Bewitch Break Inn

Potions, Poison, and Pumpkin Spice
Jingle Bells and Wedding Spells

SPIRITED SWEETS MYSTERIES
Bittersweet Betrayal
Decadent Demise
Red Velvet Revenge
Sugared Suspect

WITCH IN TIME
Better Witch Next Time
Play for Time
Time Will Tell

BEAUTY SECRETS SERIES
Makeup & Murder
Kiss & Makeup
Eyeliner & Alibis
Pedicures & Prejudice
Beauty & Bloodshed
Charm & Deception

A DROP DEAD ***Famous Cozy Mystery***
Mourning After

About the Author

Stephanie Damore is a USA Today bestselling mystery author with a soft spot for magic and romance, too. She loves being on the beach, has a strong affinity for the color pink (especially in diamonds and champagne), and, not to brag, but chocolate and her are in a pretty serious relationship.

Her books are fun and fearless, and feature smart and sassy sleuths. If you love books with a dash of romance and twist of whodunit, you're going to love her work!

For information on new releases and fun giveaways, visit her Facebook group: Paranormal Mystery Coven

https://www.facebook.com/groups/213139283675694

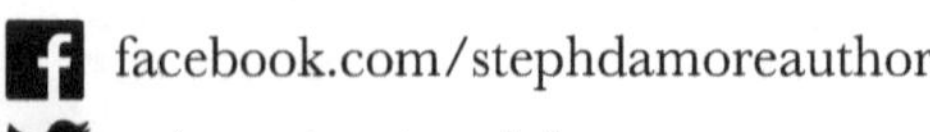

facebook.com/stephdamoreauthor

twitter.com/stephdamore

instagram.com/steph_damore_author

bookbub.com/profile/stephanie-damore